THE REAL KINGS OF CLEVELAND 2

KALITA STOKES

TEXT UCP TO 22828 TO SUBSCRIBE TO OUR
MAILING LIST
If you would like to join our team, submit the first 3-4
chapters of your completed manuscript to
Submissions@UrbanChapterspublications.com

*I would like to **dedicate** this book to my beautiful and intelligent daughter, Aurrion, and son, Wayne. You two are the best things that's ever happened to me, and God broke the mold when He made the two of you. You give me life and the strength to continue on when I don't think I can. I love you and dedicate the success of this book to you.*

ACKNOWLEDGMENTS

I would like to acknowledge my siblings; Tonda, Eric, Michelle, and my brother from another mother, Cleve.

I want to acknowledge my niece, Camille, who introduced me to the world of urban literature when she suggested I read a book written by Jahquel J. That day changed my life for the better in so many ways, so I would like to say, thank you.

I finally would like to acknowledge my sister, Nydia, for helping me realize my own potential and strength. Thanks for giving me the motivation I needed to finish book two.

Make sure you follow me on social media!
www.facebook.com/kalita.stokes
www.facebook.com/kalita.stokes.5
www.instagram.com/authork_stokes

Be sure to join my reader's group on Facebook!
Kalita's Reading Corner

1

DR. BENNETT HOWARD

Bennie

I COULDN'T EVEN FINISH my sentence because Sam walked into the room and straight up to our dear old pops, raised a nice ass 9mm, and she shot him three times in his chest, three times in his stomach, and a one-hitta-quitta shot to the head, right between his eyes, just like I taught her. My sister came in, fucked some shit up, and then dropped the muthafuckin' mic.

Afterward, Sam stood in the same place for about five minutes, staring at our dead father, before she walked over to King and attempted to wrap her arms around his waist so he could console her, but King curved her and continued pacing the floor. She looked over at me with tears running down her face, silently asking *what's going on?* I just shook my head from side to side, letting her know she should let the shit go for now, but she wouldn't be Sam if she would've done that. I knew then shit was about to go left, and I prayed I didn't have to fucking shoot King for putting his hands on my sister.

"King, can you explain to me how not even an hour ago, we were fucking in your office, and now you don't want me to touch you?" she angrily asked. King stopped pacing, turned, and looked at her with so much disgust and anger in his eyes and face—in a way he looked possessed.

"Sam, I suggest you leave, and let me calm the fuck down!" King screamed in her face with spittle landing on her face while pointing at the door.

I walked over and stood between the two, with my back to King and my chest to Sam, blocking King from being able to touch her. I grabbed Sam by the arm and tried to guide her out of the workroom, but she snatched away from me when we were almost at the door and ran back over to King who was still pacing.

"King, what the fuck did I do, huh? What did I do?" Sam hysterically cried out.

King stopped pacing and rushed over to Sam and grabbed her by the throat, squeezing hard as fuck and yelled, "You killed my muthafuckin' seed, bitch! That's the fuckin' problem!"

"King, what the fuck is wrong with you, man!" I yelled as I charged him, knocking Sam to the floor, and catching him with a nice ass two piece. He stumbled back some, but then he recovered quickly, and we started going blow for blow, both of us causing each other a lot of damage, but we were both holding our own. I didn't want to fight King, and he didn't want to fight me, and that could be seen, because neither of us was putting a lot of power into the punches we were throwing. When he put his hands on my sister, he might as well had put his hands on me, because King was being disrespectful as fuck, so I had to fuck his disrespectful ass up.

Regardless of what Sam did or didn't do, she didn't deserve that type of treatment from nobody, especially not King. If his dumb ass would have taken the time to think about what the fuck was going on, he would have realized my father was lying through his fucking teeth.

"What the fuck are y'all in here doing? Y'all brothers, and the fuckin' enemy is outside, not in this muthafucka!" Wayne yelled as he was headed our way, and everything he said was facts.

I glanced over in Sam's direction because I noticed Romello helping her up off the floor, and King took advantage of the situation, using it to get the upper hand. He flipped my body around, so my back was to his chest, wrapped his big ass right arm around my neck, and with the free hand, he placed it on my forehead locking me into place putting me into a chokehold. I was mad as hell, trying to fight to get myself out of the death grip he had me in, and with every second passed, he increased the pressure he was using to choke me. After about sixty seconds, I could feel myself getting lightheaded, and I started to feel like I was about to pass out, due to the lack of oxygen that was going to my brain.

Wayne and Main ran over to where we were tussling, trying their best to pry King's arm from around my neck, but that nigga wasn't budging at all, and it started to feel like the chokehold was getting even tighter, instead of loosening up, every time Wayne would try to loosen his arm. My knees buckled, and I dropped down, and I landed on my knees with King still squeezing tightly. He dropped to one knee at the same time I went down, so he wouldn't have to loosen or release the grip he had around my neck.

I kept tapping his forearm trying to get him to release me, but it was like he had checked out mentally, and he couldn't hear me or feel me tapping his arm because I couldn't breathe.

Wayne shouted, "King, let that nigga go! You're going to kill him!" Wayne and Main were still trying to help me get out of the hold King had me in, but King wasn't hearing shit, and at that point, it became critical because it seemed like nobody could get him to break out of the trance-like state he was in.

Once I started seeing silver specks floating in front of me, I knew then I had approximately thirty seconds before I lost consciousness. I closed my eyes and let the darkness start to consume me, and the only thought that kept running through my mind was, *my brother is about to kill me!*

Pow! Pow! Pow! Echoed throughout the room, causing me to immediately open my eyes and look around to see where the shit was coming from. King relaxed his stance and released my neck, but when he went to stand, he pushed my whole body forward, causing me to land on my hands and knees gasping for air. He slowly began backing away from me with a crazed look on his face. Suddenly, he turned and looked at Sam with murder in his eyes like he was about to attack her again. King was acting like he was high off something, and it wasn't no damn weed, but more like cocaine or something like that.

Once King was out of the room, Wayne walked over to me and helped me up off the floor. "B, what the fuck was that about? I ain't never seen him act like that before. He's normally calm and tries to keep the peace, but he's acting like he's lost his gotdamn mind," Wayne vocalized, and I was thinking the same thing.

Once I was able to stand to my feet, I walked over to my sister and pulled her into a hug, because at that point, she was a fuckin' blubbering mess. Sam dropped the gun on the floor and started crying her eyes out on my chest, "What the fuck happened, Bennie? What did I do to make him want to hurt me like this? What the fuck did I do!" she yelled while beating my chest with her fists. I felt sorry for my sister because she had just killed our father, and instead of being happy, she had to deal with the bullshit King had just done to her.

I tightened the hug I was giving her, and in a soft tone, I reassured her, "Sam, I'm so sorry this is happening, but I'll never sit around and allow anybody hurt you in front of me ever again.

"I'm not trying to say what King did was right, but our sperm donor told us about you getting pregnant by King and aborting his child because you didn't want to have a child by him. He made it seem like you willingly had the abortion and wasn't coerced." Sam pulled away from me and looked up at my face shaking her head and saying no.

"That lying son of a bitch!" Sam bellowed out, looking at our father's dead body on the ground. She took off toward the metal bat I used to beat his ass with, picked it up off the floor, and started beating my father's dead corpse repeatedly. With every blow she rendered to his body, Sam yelled out things that I could tell she'd been holding in for a long.

"I fucking hate you, you piece of shit! *Pow!* I hate you for every time you beat my ass! *Pow!* For every time you beat my mother's ass! *Pow!* I wish I would have killed you a long time ago, bitch! And have fun in hell!" After she said that, she continued reigning blows with the bat, but she stopped saying obscenities with every swing. All she did was grunt every time the bat contacted Max's body.

Wayne started walking toward her to stop her, but I signaled for him to let her be. She needed to get the pent-up aggression she had been holding in forever, out. *If it took her beating our father's corpse with a bat to help her get over the torture she endured at the hands of our father, so be it,* I thought.

I signaled for Wayne and Romello to walk over to me so I could let them know what needed to be done. "Mello, once we're through here, I need for you to take Sam to Damien's, or she may want to just go home. Walk her to the door and make sure she gets inside and you hear the locks turn," I ordered, and Mello nodded his head, letting me know he understood my instructions.

"Can y'all give us some privacy, and one of y'all call cleanup so they can clean this shit up, ASAP?"

"Yeah. I'll call cleanup once I leave out of here," Wayne responded. He, Main, and Mello walked out of the workroom, leaving just me and Sam by ourselves with our father's dead body.

I took a few slow steps toward Sam, and when she raised the bat to hit our father, I caught the bat mid-swing as she was bringing it down on Max's body. She looked at me like she was possessed, but she didn't move, and when she realized what was going on, she broke down and started bawling her eyes out.

"Shhh, shhh. Sis, it's okay... I got you. That mutha-fucka can't hurt either one of us again. I love you, and I got you, Sam," I said as I removed the bat from her hands and pulled her into my chest, hugging the life out of her. Sam's knees buckled, and I was glad I was holding her as tight I was because it prevented her body from falling to the floor.

"Shhh. It's OK, Sam. Let that shit out. Let it out, baby girl," I said as I continued rubbing her back, trying to soothe her. As I comforted her, it made me think about the shit my father said regarding Sam. I knew it might not have been a good time to ask her about what our father did to her, but I just had to know the truth. "Sam, I need to talk to you about something our father said happened in the past, and I need for you to tell me the truth... Did Max ever touch you sexually in any way while we were growing up? I promise this won't leave this room, but the stuff he said to King and I hinted toward something like that." Sam started crying harder than before. Her body started shaking, and after a couple of minutes like that, she pulled away from me and looked me in the eyes. She had snot mixed with tears running down her face, and the reluctance in her eyes made me regret even asking her the question.

"God, why? Why would you put me through all of that? I was a child, and he destroyed me!" Sam screamed at the top of her lungs, while looking up at the ceiling. I'd never seen Sam act like that before. It was like she was having a mental breakdown right in front of me, and my heart broke for my little sister.

"Ben... Bennie... He did a lot of terrible things to me, repeatedly... to the point where I lost count of how many times he violated me. He did things a father should never do to their child. He—"

I cut her off because I didn't need the details, I just wanted to know if he had really done the sick shit he told me and King he did. I didn't need to know how far he took things, because regardless of how far he took the situation, when he looked at his child in a sexual manner, that was crossing the line in my book.

"Wait! You said you *and* King?" Sam pointed out suddenly, while looking into my eyes and awaiting my response.

"Yeah," I affirmed.

"Fuck!" Sam screamed, and her voice echoed off the walls, making her screams magnified.

Sam sat down in one of the chairs and stayed quiet for a few minutes, and then she confided in me about what happened at the hands of our father. "I know you said you didn't want me to give you the details, but I've never disclosed to anyone this part of the abuse I endured." Sam paused and looked down at her hands like they would give her the strength she needed to confide in me. After about five minutes, she started talking.

"When I was younger, our father molested me. He would touch me inappropriately and have me perform disgusting acts on him... Exactly three weeks after he forced me to abort me and King's child, he started raping me, and it went on throughout my entire junior and senior year of high school." The tears were running like a faucet down her face, and she kept using the bottom of her shirt to wipe her tears away.

"Damn, Sam! I'm sorry, ma... If I knew that shit was

going on, I would have killed his ass after the first time he raped you. Did our mother know what he was doing to you?" I questioned because I was curious to know if our mother knew her pedophile ass husband was doing that nasty shit?

"Honestly, Ben, I don't know—I know I should have said something, but he threatened to kill our mother if I ever said anything, so I kept quiet and dealt with it... What did I ever do to deserve what he did to me, Bennie?"

"Sam, you didn't do shit, and you'll never be able to make sense of the sick shit he did, so don't even try. You're not at fault for this; *he is!*" I yelled while pointing at our pops. "You did what you had to do to survive, and you got out of there as soon as you could. Something was wrong with him mentally, because that's the only way I can see how any man could do the things he did to all of us. C'mere." I pulled Sam into my chest and hugged her until she calmed down completely.

"Sam, we can leave all the fucked-up shit he did to us growing up in this room when we walk out of that door and never speak on it again," I uttered while pointing to the door to the workroom. "And you better not shed another tear for that bitch or the situation we were placed in as defenseless kids... OK?"

"Bennie, I won't, and I refuse to let him win," Sam proclaimed. She turned and gave me a long hug before standing to her feet walking toward the door. Before she turned the knob to walk out of the door, she turned and said, "Brother, thank you. I love you, and I'll talk to you tomorrow. I'm going to have one of the guys run me by Camille's to grab my stuff, and then I'll have them take me home." With that, Sam walked out of the workroom, leaving me there to battle my demons, because my blood was fuckin' boiling.

Over the years, my father was a dirty muthafucka, and he did some unthinkable things, but never in a million years did I think he would've sexually assaulted my sister. He made me do things, that I've never spoken of, to and with women for his own sexual gain. The pain in my sister eyes had me reliving some of the painful memories I had suppressed over the years. As I sat there looking at my father's unrecognizable body, I wished I could bring his bitch ass back to life just so I could get the enjoyment of killing his ass again.

2

MRS. MONIQUE HOWARD

Moe

I WAS in a good ass sleep when Camille barged into the guestroom and woke me up, asking me if I knew where Sam ran off to, because she couldn't find her. I had no clue because I had been asleep since last night, just like Camille was. We searched and called around trying to find out where she was, and when we went down to the kitchen to make us some coffee, we found a letter from Sam that stated she went home last night, but she didn't include an explanation of why.

Sam wrote in the letter that she didn't want to disturb our sleep to tell us that she was leaving, and that was the reason behind writing the letter. I was glad she didn't because over the last couple of weeks I was having the hardest time falling asleep at night and staying asleep. The times I did fall asleep, I would have nightmares about shit from my past and end up waking up and not being able to fall back to sleep. So the sleep I did get, was much needed and gave me life.

Since we knew Sam was safe, I decided to just head home and go spend some much-needed quality time with my husband since our time together had been limited. We had an appointment with our family therapist, Dr. Kelly Winters later that evening so we could work on getting our marriage back on track because we were really struggling since our children passed away.

The day we buried them, I felt like a part of my heart was ripped out of my chest and buried in the casket with them, and I'd been struggling daily trying to cope with their deaths. I think I blamed myself for causing their deaths because I was the one driving the car that crashed, ending my babies' lives. I failed them, because I was supposed to protect them from harm and hurt; and I didn't do that.

Bennie had also been on my mind since I had woken up that morning, and that was the reason I had been speeding since I pulled out of Camille's driveway. I was worried about my husband because I had been calling and texting him all morning, and he didn't return any on my phone calls, nor did he respond to any of my text messages. That wasn't like Bennie. He always answered my calls, unless he was in a position where he couldn't, but then he would call me back right away. So I'd been worried about him since I opened my eyes.

As I pulled into our driveway, nothing seemed out of place, so I hit the button that opened the garage door, and once it raised all the way up, I pulled my car into my parking space. My eyes immediately looked to where Bennie normally parked his car, and when I saw Bennie's

2017 all-midnight-blue Porsche Cayenne in his parking space, I immediately calmed down some. I couldn't calm down completely until I laid my eyes on him and made sure he was okay. Shit had been mad crazy for him lately since he had to take on more responsibilities with KDB, due to King taking some much-needed time off to grieve KJ's death.

Bennie and I still hadn't been sexually active since I returned home from Africa, and I truly believed Bennie was having trouble being intimate with me because of the rape. Ever since the day I told him about what his father did to me, he'd been acting funny around me and distant as hell. I could be sitting right in front of him, but it was like he didn't see me or acknowledge me. I would have to initiate interactions between us, especially sexually.

The extent of our sexual contact had been kissing and me rubbing and touching him, but anything past that, he would shut the shit down if I tried to initiate sexual inter-course. I didn't know what else to do, and I hoped Kelly could really help us, because I didn't know how much more rejection I could take from him.

I finally made it into the house and walked upstairs and into my bedroom, where Bennie was asleep with the covers draped over his body, and my attention was pulled straight to his morning wood. His rod lay underneath the thin sheet forming a tent, and in my mind, his dick was waving at me, saying, *come and get me.*

While I walked toward the bed, naughty thoughts invaded my mind, and when I pulled the sheet down and off his body, my excitement grew. The head of his dick was hanging out of the slit in his boxers, and my mouth watered in anticipation of the naughty things I was about to do with it. I knew Bennie wasn't comfortable being intimate with me, but I couldn't help myself because I needed my husband, just as much as I knew he needed me.

I hovered over his body for a few seconds before bending down and licking the tip of his penis a few times nice and slow. He didn't move, so I continued licking around the head, and I was enjoying every second of it. Wrapping my mouth around the entire tip of his dick, I moved my mouth up and down just the head like a Popsicle until my mouth was nice and wet. Bennie kept his eyes closed and moaned out lowly. Bennie slept extremely hard, especially when he had a long and hard day. So knowing Bennie, he probably thought he was dreaming about someone giving him head, and I better had been the woman in that dream pleasing him too.

Since my mouth was good and wet, I started taking his rod in completely, moving my mouth up and down on it, loosening my mouth and jaws, which allowed me take more of him in until my lips were able to hit the base of his dick. I stayed right there, moving my head side to side making myself gag purposely. Once the tears rolled down my face, I knew I was pushing my limits, so I slid him completely out of my mouth allowing the buildup of saliva drip down on his long and thick ten-inch dick, making it look like a Popsicle.

I started going in on his dick, bobbing and weaving, moving my mouth up and down his dick all a while applying the exact amount of suction my husband liked. Bennie started coming out of his coma, slightly moaning and stirring in his sleep. You would think as hard as he slept and how hard it was to wake him, that it would hard for his dick to get an erection, but that wasn't the case, because if I blew on "my best friend", it would rise to the occasion.

I sucked his penis back in my mouth, and once I got a good rhythm going, I wrapped my hand around his dick at the base and used it to chase my mouth. As I went up and down, my hand did the same, while using a twisting method for added pleasure. "Oh, shit. This feels good as fuck, Moe," Bennie moaned out. When I looked up, we made eye contact, and the sexual hunger in his eye told a story of their own.

Ben grabbed the sides of my face with both hands and started to forcefully push my head up and down on his dick at a pace he felt was suitable. It was a little fast, but I fully accepted the challenge. I was multitasking like a muthafucka—gagging, bobbing, twisting, and playing with his balls with my free hand.

"Tighten those jaws up, ma," he ordered, and I obliged and tightened my jaws as much as I could. "Fuckkk... Yeah, just like that, baby girl... Fuck!" Bennie bellowed out again. I could tell he was about to cum because he started talking dirty, and his dick began throbbing in my mouth, causing me to close my eyes and take pleasure in pleasing my husband. "Ma... I'm about to nut, and I want you to swallow every last drop, okay?" I guess I didn't respond fast enough because he forcibly used my hair to pull my head, causing me to immediately open my eyes and look him.

"Did you fuckin' hear me?" I nodded my head without releasing the suction my jaws had around him, and he began pumping into my mouth at a fast pace.

Four pumps later, he came all in my mouth, and his sweet nut slid down my throat. I continued to suck him off until I stopped feeling his cum shooting in my mouth. "Moe, stick your tongue out, and let me see it," Bennie requested. I had already swallowed most of it, but I left just a little on my tongue because I knew his freaky ass liked to see it on my tongue.

I stuck my tongue out so he could see it, but instead of just swallowing like I normally do I spit it back onto his dick and started sucking on his semi-erection some more until I felt I sucked all his kids out of his nut sac. "Moe, what the fuck are you doing, ma? Damn," he growled out while unable to control his movements. I finally released his dick, making a loud popping sound that echoed throughout the room.

He lay there with his eyes closed tightly, trying to catch his breath as I started to undress. When he finally opened his eyes, he noticed what I was doing and said, "Hold up, Moe... don't get undressed yet, because I need to talk to about something important, and it can't wait." That shit crushed me because I felt like he was rejecting my ass again. I didn't say anything I just pulled my shirt back over my head and sat on the side of the bed.

"Let me go in the bathroom really quick to clean up so we can talk." Bennie got out of the bed, walked into the bathroom, closed the door, and took care of his business.

I didn't want him to see the tears that were streaming from my eyes when he came out of the bathroom, so I turned my back to the bathroom door when I lay down in the bed.

Moments later, I heard the door open, and I became extremely nervous for some reason. I guess it was because I didn't know what he wanted to tell me. I felt the opposite side of the bed sink in some, and moments later, I felt my husband crawl up behind me, and he pulled me into a spooning position, which he knew I loved. I closed my eyes and relished in the moment of how good it felt lying in his arms, causing memories of the good times to flood my mind.

"Baby, I love the fuck out of you so much, and I've been waiting a long time to be able to have this conversation with you," Bennie whispered softly in my ear after he kissed it.

"What conversation have you been waiting to have with me?" I asked curiously, sniffling and wiping the tears from my eyes.

"Baby... Max is dead! The nightmare we've been living through, because of him, is over. He won't ever be able to hurt you or anybody else I love again," Bennie stated with a tone laced with happiness for the first time I'd heard in a while.

I began analyzing what he said. I released the breath I didn't even know I was holding, and tears started rolling down onto the pillow I was laying on. I truly didn't know how to feel about what he said, but my soul felt lighter knowing his father couldn't hurt anyone else. I'd been dreaming about how I would jump for joy when I found out he was dead, but with the way my marriage had been going, it made the news Bennie just shared bittersweet. Then I was also scared for my husband because I didn't know how killing his father would eventually affect Bennie mentally.

"Babe, say something please," Bennie begged, because initially, I didn't respond because I didn't know what to say. I had so many questions I wanted answered, but I didn't think it was the right time to be prodding Bennie for play-by-play details of how he killed his father.

"Baby, I don't know what you want me to say right now because it's a lot to take in all at once. Yes, I'm happy he's dead, but I'm also concerned with how all of this will affect you... and honestly Sam. This man has violated so many people in so many ways, but he was still your father at the end of the day... How do you feel about him being dead?" I asked, rolling over so I could look my husband in his eyes while he expressed his feelings.

I started rubbing the back of his head. He closed his eyes, and I could feel his body relax against mine. "I'm glad he's dead, and now we can try to focus on our marriage, not the bullshit he caused from our past. I love you, and I want our marriage to work. I think once we start therapy, we'll be able to discuss it in more depth, the things that we need to work on as a married couple, and the things we need to work on individually. I don't want you worrying about me though, because I'm OK. What I need you to focus on is making sure you're mentally good."

"All I can say is I'll try my best." I looked over at the clock on my nightstand and realized we only had only an hour or so before our scheduled therapy appointment. "Babe, I think we should start getting ready because we have only a little over an hour to make it to our appointment on time." With that, Bennie went into his closet to find him something to wear, and I went into the bathroom and started taking a shower.

I turned the showerhead on and adjusted the knob so

the setting was on the temperature I liked. Once the temperature was to my liking I climbed into the shower, and my mind immediately started racing.

After about ten minutes of my allowing the water to wash over my body, I concluded that Bennie wasn't going to join me. I just assumed since he allowed me to give him oral sex that he was starting to accept what his father did to me, and we were moving in a positive direction, especially since he allowed me to give him oral sex. See, that was my problem with Bennie—his actions didn't match what came out of his mouth.

We both said we wanted our marriage to work out, but the last couple of weeks, Bennie had been acting weird to me, and I felt like it was more than what happened with his father. Don't get me wrong, I had been trying to take into consideration everything that was going on, but it felt like something else was going on.

"Mr. and Mrs. Howard, Dr. Winters is ready to see you now. Can you please follow me, and I'll escort you to her office?" Dr. Winters's secretary said before Bennie and I followed her back to Kelly's office. Once inside the office, Kelly motioned for us to have a seat on the couch, and once I was seated, I couldn't wait to speak.

"Hello, Bennett and Monique. Would you like anything to drink before we get started? I have water, coffee, and tea," Dr. Winters asked.

Simultaneously, we both said, "No."

Kelly started the session off. "Well, I talked to Monique briefly about some issues you're having when she scheduled this therapy appointment. In your own words, Bennett, what brings the two of you in today?" Dr. Winters asked. We both looked at one another, and he didn't say a word. Since Bennie didn't say anything, she turned to me asked me a question trying to get the conversation started.

"Well, Monique, how did your last stint volunteering abroad go? Did it help you establish some tools you can use to help you deal with the issues you have related to the accident and everything else surrounding it?" Kelly questioned. See, when I came for my private therapy session earlier that week, I told Kelly about the rape, and I told her who the rapist was, so she knew a lot already about what was going on in our marriage. I assumed she was just trying to get me to come clean to Bennie, but little did she know, I had already told him, but I just hadn't had a chance to let her know that.

"Well... I finally told Bennett about the rape. My issue is, ever since I told him, he's been treating me differently. I feel like he looks at me like I'm tarnished or spoiled goods. I believe that's why he doesn't want me sexually anymore. If you take the sexual aspect out of it, the intimacy we used to share is nonexistent, and I don't know if I can live like this anymore. Bennie, you don't hold me, kiss me, or even tell me why and how much you love me. Then add to the mix that we haven't had sex in over four months, which was before I went abroad, and I don't know what else to do. Like today, he allowed me to perform oral sex on him, but afterward, he didn't want to have sex with me.

"Even if it's just a kiss, he looks so uncomfortable, and I don't know what to do. I truly feel like when he thinks about having sex with me, it disgusts him," I cried out because I felt an overwhelming feeling of emotions telling her how I really felt about everything.

Kelly looked back and forth between the both of us, and it seemed like she was waiting to see if Bennie would respond, but he didn't. "Well, Bennett, how do you feel about what Monique just said?" Dr. Winters asked. You could tell he was thinking hard on what he wanted to say and how he wanted to say it.

"Dr. Winters, I wholeheartedly love my wife, imperfections and all, but I'm having a hard time looking at her in a sexual way right now." Bennie paused and looked down at his hands before speaking again. "I was supposed to protect my family from harm, and instead of protecting them, I failed them all, and I hate myself for that... I took pride in knowing that my wife saved herself for me, and to know I'm not the only man she had sex with... I've been battling with knowing I'm not the only man to have her in that way, and to know it was my father makes it even harder for—"

I cut him off before he could finish what he was saying. "Bennie, it's not my fault your father violated me, beat me, and made me do terrible things to him. I didn't ask for this shit!" I didn't cry, which surprised me. I stood and was about to walk out of the door, but Bennie pulled me back down on the couch.

"Damn, Moe! I'm not blaming you for what he did to you. It's just hard, and I'm trying my best to get past this shit. He hurt you and violated you, and I wasn't there to stop it from happening, and my kids... my kids are dead because of the shit he did to you," Bennie sadly said. I noticed he had tears rolling down his cheeks, so I wiped them away, but more replaced them. It made me so sad knowing how bad he was struggling with all of this, and there was really nothing I can do to help him get through it.

"Moe, baby, I'm not disgusted by you, but I'm disgusted with the situation." I could tell by the way Bennie was looking like it was more he wanted to say.

Kelly took the words right out of my mouth when she said, "Bennie, if you want this to work, you must be completely honest with Monique." You could tell he was battling with if he really wanted to tell me the truth or keep it to himself.

"Moe, I haven't touched you sexually because every time I touch you, thoughts of my father raping you invade my mind, and no matter what I do, it doesn't change a damn thing. That's why I haven't been able to have sex with you... I want you so bad, but I can't get out of my head. Just like this morning, it took everything in me not to come join you in the shower, but I didn't because I didn't want to make things worse," Bennie explained, and his statement didn't surprise me at all, because that was how I'd been feeling for the longest.

Kelly interjected, "Well, let me start out by saying this. Bennett, what you're experiencing is normal. A lot of spouses that have wives that's been raped go through the exact same thing your experiencing right now. I don't want you to beat yourself up, because it's not wrong for you to feel that way, so don't be too hard on yourself, please. I have a question I would like the both of you to answer; do you want your marriage to work, and if you do, are you willing to put in the work it'll take to get back on track?" Dr. Winters asked the both of us.

I didn't even hesitate when I answered the question. "Yes, I want my marriage to work, but I can't continue to live like this. We've lost so much over the last couple of years, and the devastation of losing our children did a number on us and left us both emotionless." I turned to Bennie and said, "I just know I don't want to lose you, and honestly, I don't think I would survive it if I did."

"Babe, you're not going to lose me. We just have to work hard to get things back on track. Dr. Winters, I want my marriage, and I'm willing to do whatever it takes to make it work," Bennie vowed. He grabbed my hand and kissed the back of it so softly.

The other thing that concerned me was the baby aspect of things. I wanted to know how Kelly felt about it, so I asked her, "Dr. Winters, do you think it would be best to start trying to have another child right now?"

"That's a tricky question to answer because considering the situation, that question can be answered multiple ways. I'll state the obvious first—you must be intimate to get pregnant. I think you and Bennett lost yourselves when your children passed away, and I think for your marriage to work, you must find what you lost in order to get that spark back. My suggestion for you two is to start over and rebuild your foundation, and this time, make it stronger than before.

"Bennett, start over and court your wife again. Go on some date nights, long walks, long talks, and make her fall in love with you again. I think you'll know if the time is right to start trying to have a child together. My only request is don't rush things," the doctor ordered, and I looked over at my husband and started blushing.

We continued to talk for about another twenty

minutes. She gave us homework, which was we had to replicate our first date. Whoever planned our first date in college had to plan it this time also. Kelly also told us to keep things light and simple and without expectations.

We walked out of that appointment hand in hand, and I finally felt optimistic that maybe we could really save our marriage. Maybe everything would work out as long we put in the hard work and dedicate the time into reconciling anything was possible. I just prayed there wasn't anything out there lingering that could potentially throw a monkey wrench in our reconciliation. I believed we only had one shot left at getting things right and saving our marriage.

3

DR. SAMANTHA HOWARD

Sam

WHEN I WOKE up the next morning, I was still in disbelief of what happened the night before. It wasn't enough that my father ruined my entire childhood, but he decided to take it up a notch and destroy my fucking future with King with the lies he told surrounding me aborting our baby. Regardless of what King and I went through, he should have known I would have never aborted our child unless I was forced to do it. King believing the lies my father told saddened me more than him putting his hands on me.

I knew King told me to wait in his office and he would send someone up to get me when they were ready for me to come down and handle my father, but when I saw everyone leaving the conference room and walk over to the workroom, I became really antsy. It seemed like it was taking forever, so I took it upon myself to go downstairs to the workroom and end the shit. I lied to the workers once I got down there and told them King called up to his office and told me to come down. They didn't even question it. They just unlocked the workroom door for me so I could go inside.

As I entered the room and saw my father hanging from the ceiling, beaten and bleeding out, I started having flashbacks of all the times he abused me, raped me, and tortured me. I never told anyone about my father raping me because I was too scared and embarrassed. He raped me my entire junior and senior year of high school. The first time was six weeks after I aborted King's baby, and I remember the sick shit like it was yesterday.

"Don't scream... If you do, I'll kill you and your mother," *my father said to me as I was jolted from a deep sleep with his hand covering my mouth and his body on top of mine, anchoring me down. Initially, I tried to fight against him, but he was too heavy, and I even tried to scream at the top of my lungs, even with his hand covering my mouth. But once he threatened to kill me and my mother, I stopped because I knew he would follow through with his threat.*

I nodded my head so he would know I understood, and a sadistic smile crept upon his face. He kept one hand over my mouth and ripped my panties off with his other hand. The tears started pouring out of my eyes, and the fear was leaking from my pores, because I didn't understand how my father could do something so disgusting to his own daughter. I began shaking my head side to side, trying to let him know I didn't want him to do it, but it seemed like it excited him even more.

"You know you want this just like I do," *he said to me as he stuck one of his fingers inside me. I was dry as a bone, so he*

removed his finger, put it in my mouth to wet it, but before he stuck the finger in me, he said, "You better get wet because it's going to hurt worse if you don't." All I could think about was the abortion and how I didn't want him to cause more damage to my body if he had sex with me and I was dry. At that point, I made the conscious decision to close my eyes and act like it was King I was having sex with and not my father raping me.

"Yeah, I knew you wanted me. See how wet you're getting for Daddy." He kept saying that shit, and it made me throw up in my mouth a little bit.

He removed his finger, opened my legs wider, and entered me roughly. I kept my eyes closed almost the entire time he pumped in and out of me feverishly while I cried like a newborn baby. The way his breath smelled made my stomach churn, and the way he kept grunting the entire time he pumped in and out of me made my ears ache. I begged him to stop, but my words were muffled by his hand, and even if his hand wasn't there and he could hear my cries he would have continued with the assault. "I love you so much, Sammie. I want you to have my baby, and you better want it like you did King's." My eyes popped opened, and I started feverishly trying to push him off me because that was the sickest shit I had ever heard. He came inside of me after about four or five more pumps. After he was done, he laid there with his penis still inside me pulsating.

When he finally got up, I asked him, "Why? Why would you do this to your daughter? Why do you hate me so much?" He looked at me for a few minutes without saying a word, and then he started grabbing his clothes off the floor and putting them back on.

He walked over to the door, and before he walked out, he

turned and said, "Don't fuckin' question me. Ask your mother."
With that, he walked out.

After he left my room, I took a scalding-hot shower and cried myself to sleep, but it was that type of sleep where your barely sleep. Every noise I heard made me jump up because I was scared he was going to come back in my room and rape me again.

The next morning when I woke up, I went to the John Glen Health Center—the free clinic—and got a Plan-B pill and some birth control pills that I took my birth control faithfully every day because he had me fucked up if he thought I would have a baby by him.

From that point on, my father violated me every chance he could, maybe two to three times per week, and it was nothing I could do about it without getting somebody I truly loved hurt, so I just dealt with it until I could get out.

That's why when I walked into the workroom, I let my gun rip like that. I let it rip for all the mental, physical, and emotional abuse he caused me, and it felt so damn good. The feelings that ran through my body when I pulled that muthafuckin' trigger empowered me, knowing I was the cause of him taking his last breath. I was finally able to take back my innocence, back my life that he ripped away from me all those years ago. But that feeling was short-lived when King started choking the hell out of me. For King to believe what that muthafucka said hurt me to the core, and it made me question what type of man King really was.

He knew me better than anyone, and he knew there was no way in hell I would have killed our child if I had any choice in the matter. Yeah, I should've told King back then about the pregnancy, and if I could go back in time, I would've told him, but I thought I was protecting him from feeling the hurt and pain over losing a child like I was experiencing, and I was struggling mentally knowing I had killed our innocent baby.

I was at such a low point post abortion that I contemplated suicide for a week straight, thinking of all the different ways I could kill myself. I thought about hanging myself, slitting my wrist, pills, and poison, but the only thing that stopped me from doing it was my stubbornness and resilience. If I would have killed myself, my father would have won, and I wasn't about to let that happen. His number-one goal in life was to break me, Bennie, and my mother, and I refused to allow his actions to continue to hurt me and hold me back from being the best me I could be. That's why instead of killing myself to get out, I devised a plan to get out that wouldn't cause me any harm. I knew the only way to get away from my father was to get a scholarship and go far away to college.

I knew at an early age, I wanted to be a doctor, and I knew for me to get the type of scholarship I needed, I had to get it for my academics because I didn't play any sports. I threw myself into my studies and registered for some college courses at Tri-C Community College. It gave me an excuse to spend more time away from home, and it helped guarantee me a full ride to Harvard. My father wasn't happy at first when I told him about me taking college courses while still in high school, but I just told him it was required for me to graduate, and his dumb ass believed me.

It was crazy because even though I hated my father, I

expected him to come to at least come to my high-school graduation or be proud of me when I graduated top of my class and because I received a full ride to one of the most prestigious colleges like Harvard. Nope, not his jealous ass. Like I was the reason his father pulled him out of school while he was in the fifth grade to run the family business. He also hated the fact I was going to school out of state and would finally be able to get away from his controlling and abusive ass, but I was so happy that I was finally getting out, and I had already decided once I left, I would never return to that hellhole called home, and my father knew once I walked out of that door, he would never see me again.

That's why the day I left for college was one of the best days of my life, even though my father was on one from the time I opened my eyes that morning until the cab picked me up to drop me off at the Greyhound bus station. He kept nitpicking so he could stir up arguments with my mother, but I refused to be pulled into his bull-shit, so I stayed in my room until it was time for me to get picked up.

When the cab blew its horn, alerting me of its arrival, I grabbed all my stuff and headed downstairs where my mother and father were sitting. If looks could kill, I would have gone up in fucking flames because my father had so much hate in his eyes, and it didn't help that I had a big ass Kool-Aid smile on my face.

Once I walked out onto the porch, I knew it was now or never if I wanted to tell my father how I really felt about all the abuse I suffered at his hands. I knew I would be safe from him hurting me for speaking my mind because we were on the front porch, and a lot of people had already gathered in front of our house to see me off to school. I knew my father would never want the outside world to know and see how much of an animal he really was and what he had been doing behind closed doors. I turned to my father and told him how I really felt about everything he did to me over the years.

"All my life you hated me and never had a clue why. You were supposed to be my protector and keep me safe from harm, but instead of the world hurting me, you did. You made it your point in life to make my life a living hell, and that you did succeed in doing. You broke my mother, Bennie, and you almost broke me, but I want you to know I might have swayed from time to time, but your weak ass didn't break me. I'm going to go to school and strive to graduate top of my class. I will be a doctor, but you'll never get a chance to experience seeing your only daughter save lives. This is the last time you'll ever see me, and I truly hope you die a long, miserable ass death, bitch."

I turned to my mom and said, "Mom, I don't know if you knew this or not, but your sick ass husband is a pedophile, and he has been raping me for the last two years. He has beaten me countless times, which I know you know about, but I pray you didn't know he was violating me and didn't do anything about it. I hope you get the courage one day to leave his miserable ass and get a chance to have real life and happiness."

When I looked around, it was a few of our neighbors standing around with their hands covering their mouth, looking like they were in shock from what I had just revealed about my father. My father rushed into the house because he was embarrassed because his secrets were out, and he knew things would never be the same for him. That was the last time I saw my mother alive, and I hated that, because regardless of what I went through, I really did love my mother, but I just hated how she allowed my father to mistreat me and Bennie. My mother died before I ever got the chance to ask her about the letter she snuck into my luggage before I left for school.

4

Sam

*RING! **Ring! Ring!*** My phone ringing pulled me out of my thoughts, but I allowed it to continue ringing until the voicemail picked up the call. I didn't want to answer the phone because I wasn't ready to talk to anyone. I grabbed my phone and checked to see if I missed a call or text from Nina since Kassidy was with her. As I scrolled through, I had a million text messages from Moe, Camille, and even Bennie asking me if I was okay? *Hell no, I'm not okay, but eventually, this too shall pass, and this too will be just a bad memory,* I thought.

I sent everyone an *I'm okay* text and put my phone back on my nightstand so I could empty my bladder and take a hot shower before I returned any phone calls.

Once I finished using the bathroom, I washed my hands and then turned on the showerheads so the water could warm up to the temperature of my liking. When I looked in the mirror, I got the shock of my life. King's handprints were embedded into my skin, covering the entire front of my neck, and the bruise jumped out at me because my skin was so light. The bruising was purple and red in color, and it was so sore to the touch. *That nigga really tried to choke me out,* I thought as I traced the marks with my fingers. The sadness overwhelmed me completely, and I broke down into a much-needed cry on the bathroom floor.

Never in a million years did I ever think King would hurt me like that, especially after we had just had sex in his office less than an hour before. I thought we had finally broken through whatever barriers were preventing us from being together, but I guess not.

I remained on the floor and cried until the tears dried up and there was no more to replace the ones that had already fallen. I picked myself up from the floor, jumped into the shower, and let the steaming hot water run from the top of my head, down my body, and down the drain. I wished my problems would've run down the drain like the water, but that was wishful thinking.

After about five minutes, I grabbed my washcloth, washed my face twice, and then soaped up my washcloth with my Dove liquid body wash. As I lathered my body, memories of what me and King shared in his office the night before started rushing back with a vengeance. I closed my eyes and fantasized about the way he touched and caressed my body, how soft his fingertips felt on my skin, how his cologne invaded my nostrils, how the smell was embedded in my clothes and body last night, and the way he fucked the shit out of me on the couch in his office.

Before I knew it, my hand was rubbing my clit slowly in a circular motion. In my mind, I imagined it being King's fingers bringing me so much pleasure and joy, as my other hand and fingers grabbed, pinched, and twisted my nipples, and within about thirty seconds, the flood-gates opened, bringing me to an orgasmic state. My breaths were heavy, heartbeat racing, and womanly parts aching as I lathered my washcloth again so I could clean myself. I quickly washed up, rinsed my body, jumped out of the shower, and grabbed a towel to dry myself off.

When I walked back into my bedroom, I immediately grabbed my phone off my nightstand to call Camille, because I needed to vent about what happened the night before and possibly get some advice on what I should do about King. Even though he choked me, I still loved the nigga's dirty drawers. I unlocked my phone and dialed her number, and as the phone rang, I placed it on speaker so I could still use my hands during the call.

Camille answered on the third ring going the hell off on me. "Bitch, don't you ever do no shit like that to me again, OK!" Camille screamed through the phone. "You just left and didn't wake me up and say shit. This morning after I woke up, I walked through my house looking for you, and when I couldn't find you, I thought maybe something had happened to you, Sam.

"I woke Moe up asking her if she knew where you went and found out she was just as clueless as my ass. We called around looking for your bum ass, but the entire time, you were nice and safe at home. Then you had the nerve to leave a love letter and shit on my fridge telling me you went home. Bitch, it would have been smart if you had put the letter on my fuckin' nightstand in the first place because you knew I was going to flip out when I couldn't find you, Sam.

"You know the men in our family climbing up the ladder out here in these streets, so that means they've developed enemies that will hurt us in order to hurt them," Camille expressed.

"I'm sorry, boo! I just... I just needed time to think by myself so I could analyze everything that happened last night because it was a bit much, Mill," I responded.

Camille mumbled, "It just would have decreased the stress in my already stressful ass life that's all I'm saying." She let out a loud breath before she threatened me with, "Just know I'm fucking your ass up when I see you for scaring me like that." I felt bad because my intentions were never meant to have her worrying about me. I just needed to be by myself so I could mentally decompress, and I knew Camille would've tried to figure out a way to have me talk about what happened, and I wasn't ready to talk about it at all.

Mill asked, "But anyway, what did you have to analyze? What's going on, cause your letter was really vague, and I've been wracking my brain trying to figure out what happened to you? Ooh, best friend, did you and King fuck or something?"

I didn't respond right away because I got lost in my thoughts. "Bitch, did you hear me!" Camille yelled through the phone, pulling me out of my thoughts.

"Yeah, I heard you. I was just thinking about everything that happened last night. Well, let's just say my father went out of town to visit my mother, down south, and I think he's going to permanently stay down there and not come back to Cleveland." That was my code basically saying, that nigga pushing up daisies. "Before my father left, he told King that when I was sixteen, I found out I was pregnant by him, and I told him I wanted an abortion because I didn't want to have King's baby. Mill, other than my mother, you're the only person that knew I was even pregnant, and you know I wanted to keep my baby. I didn't want to kill my child. I wanted to keep my baby and raise him with King, and for him to believe the bullshit my father said is eating me up inside. King should know me better than that, Mill," I cried out.

"Listen, Sam, I'm your friend, and we both know we can't do shit but keep it real with one another, even if we don't want to hear it. I still must tell you the truth. Our honesty with one another is one of the reasons why we've been friends for so long, and that's why our bond is so tight. I told you back then you should have told him before Max forced you to abort y'all baby. Even if you still ended up having the abortion, he deserved to know and have a say in what happened. I told you that secrets like this always find a way of coming to the light. I love you, but you were dead ass wrong, best friend."

"You don't understand, Camille, what I went through when that monster found out I was pregnant... The night I left your house after taking the pregnancy test, he beat my mother's ass so bad and made me watch the entire time. It killed me hearing her scream for him to stop and for someone to help her. Then when he got tired of beating her, he took a rest and then started beating the hell out of me. He punched, kicked, and stomped me out, and all I could do was curl up in a ball and try to protect the baby the best I could," I cried out. The tears were streaming down my face, and my words kept getting stuck in my throat, making it hard for me to even tell her what happened that night.

"Sam, I'm sooo sorry you had to go through that, best friend. I didn't know how bad things were for you because you never talked to me about it." Camille's voice cracked a couple of times while she was talking, so I knew she was on the other end of the phone probably crying. When I hurt, my best friend hurt, and that was the reason I kept what I was going through at home in the dark from everyone.

"That wasn't even the worst part of it. The same day I had the abortion... My father made me break up with King and said if I told anyone about the abortion, he would kill King and my mother. That's why I ended up breaking up with him, and my father said I couldn't be friends with you anymore. He also told me I couldn't hang out with you anymore because you're the reason I was out there fucking in the first place."

Camille took in a deep breath and blew it out, but she didn't respond for about sixty seconds, and then she said, "Now it all makes sense, because the way you cut King and me off was suspect as hell, and we couldn't figure out why you did it. Are you going to tell King what really happened or let him continue believing what your father said? I like how you tried to skip over the question about y'all fucking? I'll let you tell me about that part when you're ready." Camille slightly chuckled because she knew me better than I knew myself at time, and she knew we had sex.

But her question made me think about everything I'd gone through in the past and everything I wanted in my future. Before last night, King was what I wanted in my life, in my future, but he had me questioning everything. I know I needed to tell him what happened, but at that point, I didn't know how I wanted to handle everything.

I knew I wanted to be able to maintain good health and to be happy, but I didn't know if those goals were able to be achieved with King in my life. He had too many demons he was battling, and he needed to get help with developing some tools to deal with his grief because he was becoming toxic and on the verge of doing something that couldn't be undone, no matter how hard he tried. He had been acting weird since KJ died, and we all chalked it up to him grieving, but it was something else going on with him.

"Honestly, I think I eventually will talk to him about it and tell him everything, but for right now, no. I just need to stay as far away from him as possible because I can't get past that nigga putting his gotdamn hands on me last night." Before I could say anything else, Camille started going off on the other end of the line.

"What the fuck do you mean he put his hands on you? King fucking hit you? Bitch, I'ma call and cuss his punk ass out, and then I'm going to fuck his ass up when I see him!" she screamed though the phone.

"Well, I'm assuming he was pissed from what my father so-called confessed before, you know what happened. When I walked up to him, he wrapped his hands around my throat, choking me, and I swear, for a moment there, I thought he was trying to kill me. Bitch, I started seeing stars and everything. That's how tight he was choking the life out of me, and if it wasn't for Bennie intervening, there's no telling how things would have ended for me. When he knocked King off of me, he and

King ended up going blow for blow. I was terrified because it took me back to that place when I was younger, and my father would beat us. I was so scared that I was literally standing there in shock, looking around trying to understand what was going on around me."

"Wow! I can't believe all this shit has happened, and what's really throwing me for a loop is King had the audacity to put his hands on you. Now I got to shoot the nigga in his pinky toe. Fuck cussing him out! I'm shooting his crazy ass." We both burst out laughing because she was always threatening people with that line from *Harlem Nights*, but the sad part was she would really do it.

Through the laughter, I asked, "Why you got to shoot him, Camille, and not just curse him the hell out or beat his ass?"

"Bitch, are you slow or something? You just told me he choked your ass out, and he and Bennie went at it. That nigga King crazy and nice as fuck with his hands, and that's a lethal combination. Nana ain't raise no fool, and I ain't taking no chances with his ass, so I need to move accordingly." We both burst out laughing, and when the laughs stopped, she asked seriously, "Is Bennie OK though, because Moe didn't say anything about what happened when she left a little while ago? I'm assuming she doesn't know what happened."

"Yeah, he's cool," I replied. "That's understandable, but enough about me. What's going on with you and Dame? Have you talked to him since he's been gone?"

"No. I probably won't talk to him until he comes home Tuesday. He sent me a text I guess when he landed stating he loves me, but that's a crock of shit. Love should have brought his ass home those nights he was out fuckin' other bitches, because I know Chanel ain't the only one he was out there fucking. Now I must break up our unhappy ass home getting a divorce. I know I said I wouldn't communicate with him until he came home, but I couldn't help myself last night..."

"Camille, what the fuck did you do?" I questioned after giggling to myself because Camille's a hot mess.

"Well, when I went upstairs last night, I sent him this long ass text message, letting him know how I felt, and I also let him know I'm filing for divorce. I also called my attorney's office this morning and scheduled me an appointment for Monday. He'll still be out of town, so he won't be able to try and prevent me from making it to the appointment, nor will he be here to try and talk me into canceling it."

From the first time Mill told me she wanted to file for divorce, I felt like she was moving too damn fast. I knew my girl was hurt and everything, but they had been together for too long, and they made it through so much bullshit that life had thrown at them. I had to choose my words wisely, because if I didn't, Camille would shut all the way down and wouldn't talk to me about her relationship for a very long time, with her petty ass. Yes, Camille was "The Queen of Petty".

I hesitantly said, "Camille, I think you're moving too quickly. You should never make lifelong decisions on temporary emotions, boo. Why don't you just file for legal separation first if you must file something, and then see how things go? Maybe both of you can work things out soon. Plus, you know good and damn well Dame's not going to let you go that easily. He's going to fight the divorce until his last breath, regardless of the fact he's the reason you're divorcing his cheating ass." She could act like she didn't know she was married to a fool all she wanted, but I knew the real. That's why Camille and Damien were so good together because they're crazy, and their crazy was on a whole different level. They both needed to be on some medication to level their crazy asses out.

"Listen, I hear everything you're saying, but there's no coming back from this one, Sam. He violated in the worse way having a baby with her. If his sorry ass was going to be out cheating, he could have at least worn a fuckin' rubber. There's no way in hell I can cheat, come home pregnant—with a baby that ain't his—and live to see another day. He would kill me and the fuckin' baby with his crazy ass.

"He has a whole ass son with that home-wrecking *bitch*! I can't forgive that, and I refuse to accept a child that was conceived when he was out breaking our wedding vows. Fuck Damien, Chanel, and the ugly ass little boy! And I don't want my kids around Chanel or the boy!" she screamed through the phone. Now I could have sat on that phone and told her how wrong she was, but it would have been a waste of time because she was so bullheaded.

"Alright, alright... I've told you how I feel, but I'm here to support whatever decision you make. Let me get off this phone though because I have a lot of work I need to get done before the kids get back tomorrow."

"Alright, bye then, and call me if you need anything, Sam. If you feel like having company later, call me, and I'll come over and chill with you. I don't think I want to be in this big ass house by myself."

"Okay, but how your hard ass scared of being home alone?" We both burst out laughing.

"Bitch, fuck you! I ain't scared of shit. You know what I ain't fuckin' with you, and I take back my offer of coming over your house and keeping you company." Camille didn't even give me a chance to respond before she hung up the phone in my face.

Honestly, I thought when I pulled the trigger and killed my father, that immediately it was going to bring me a sense of peace, but I was sadly mistaken because all it did was make my PTSD worse. After I murdered my father and went home, it took me a while to wind my mind and body down enough to fall asleep, and I regretted going to sleep because I started having night-mares about me killing my sperm donor.

I wished King could have been there to comfort me during that difficult time, because I really needed him. I knew King had mentally been on a downward spiral since KJ passed away, so I did have empathy for his situa-tion, but that didn't give him the right to put his hands on me, because I didn't know if I could forgive him for that weak ass shit.

5

MR. KINGSTON JAMES

King

As I dropped to one knee and wrapped my right arm around my kidnappers' necks, all I kept thinking was, kill or be killed, *and I knew I wasn't dying, so I was about to either put his ass to sleep, or I was going to snap his fuckin' neck.*

I decided to just put him to sleep because I needed to be as silent as possible so the other men standing outside of the room didn't realize I gotten the upper hand on the nigga I had in a chokehold. When I tightened the hold, I could feel him starting to pass out, and the fight he once had was starting to weaken. I knew he had maybe sixty seconds of fight left in him before he went to sleep. I just wished he would hurry up because if he hadn't gone to sleep in exactly one minute, I planned on snapping his fuckin' neck. I needed to get me and Tae out of there so we could get medical treatment.

I had never experienced no shit like that before in my

life. For some reason, I couldn't tell if what I was experiencing was reality or a memory. I was battling with myself because my mind kept flashing back and forth from the workroom to Syria where I was kidnapped and tortured. I felt like I was inside a black-and-white movie, and my life was flashing back and forth quickly, from the past to the present, and I didn't know why.

Syria was a part of my life I never really talked about with anyone, and for the most part, I tried to act like the shit never happened, because that was the hardest thing I had ever had to go through, and I was knocking hard at death's door. Not only was I kidnapped, but my kidnappers also tortured me and my former military brother, Tae. My injuries were so severe that the surgeons had to place metal plates in my pelvis and hip, due to a bullet shattering those bones.

After Tae and I were rescued, I slipped into a coma for about a month, due to all the head trauma I suffered at the hands of my kidnappers, and when I came to, Tammy and KJ were right by my side. Tammy stayed with me the entire time while I recovered overseas, up until I was able to return home and finish my physical and occupational therapy. It took me over a year to recover, and Tammy held me down the entire time, but things changed after I became a hired hitter for a man by the name of Preston Paris.

Pow! Pow! Pow! The sounds of gunshots caused me to immediately open my eyes, pulling me out of my thoughts. I looked around the room to see where the shots came from, and that's when I saw a woman standing there holding a gun down to her side. She wasn't an immediate threat, so I wasn't concerned with her, but when I looked down, I noticed the man I had in a chokehold wasn't my kidnapper at all, but it was Bennie. I immediately released the hold on him and closed my eyes trying to focus, but when I opened my eyes again it was my kidnapper. I pushed the kidnapper's body forward, and he went flying, causing him to land on his hands and knees gasping for air.

I slowly began backing away from the man, and that's when I looked to my left and saw the woman standing there still holding the gun down to her side. I closed my eyes again, and when I opened them that's when I realized the woman was Sam, but I had to get out of there before I hurt someone I loved.

I ran out of the room and out of the building, jumping into my car, trying to figure out what the fuck was going on, because my mind was playing tricks on me. I laid the driver's seat back and started taking deep breaths to slow my breathing and pulse down, which allowed the adrenaline that was running through my veins to simmer down. About five minutes later, I began to feel like myself again. In a way, I felt like I had been drugged or something, but I couldn't figure out where or when could it have happened.

After about ten minutes, I started my car and headed to the liquor store because I needed a muthafuckin' drink. Once I purchased my bottle of Henny, I headed down to the lake off Martin Luther King Jr. Drive so I could think and try to figure out what happened. I always went to the lake when I needed to clear my mind and figure shit out. That was me and Sam's spot back in the day, and when we were together, we would go there whenever we wanted privacy to just chill, talk, and sometimes, even have sex.

I took a couple of sips of Henny straight from the bottle, and the alcohol went down my throat smooth as hell. Then I took a couple of pulls from the blunt after I lit it. My whole fuckin' existence immediately mellowed out. As I looked through the windshield, I could see the water crashing up against the rocks and boulders, and that caused a mental calmness to come over my mind.

I began reflecting on the events that just happened, and clarity hit my ass like a ton of bricks, and that's when I realized how I allowed Sam's father to play my ass. I walked right into his trap and did his dirty work for him, but he only got that off because Sam never said a word about being pregnant. If I had already known about the pregnancy, I wouldn't have even reacted to his pedophile ass.

I'm not gonna to lie to you, but I was hurt as hell when he announced that Sam aborted my seed, *my fuckin' kid man!* That revelation knocked the fuckin' wind out of me because at that moment, I would have given my right arm to have KJ back, and Sam was out there killing babies and shit without giving a fuck about how I felt about my kid. *Fuck, I miss my son,* I thought as tears rolled down my cheeks.

The more I drank and smoked, the more the memories of the day I buried KJ took over my mind.

I dreaded waking up that morning because it was the day I had to bury my son, and it would be the last time I would physically see him. I felt like I was in an unawakenable nightmare, and no matter what I said or did, it wouldn't bring my son back. My heart felt so heavy, and the anxiety I was feeling was starting to become overwhelming with every minute that passed. I was completely losing my fuckin' mind as the time ran down to the start of KJ's funeral.

Every day since my son died, I tried to figure how KJ ended up dead, considering after his surgery to remove his appendix, the surgeons were very optimistic about him possibly making a full recovery. Yes, he was having some complications from the sepsis afterward, but nothing life-threatening. So when I received the call that he had passed away, I was truly confused, because I had just left the hospital, and he was stable. I guess it wasn't meant for me to understand why God decided to take him away from me.

As my black Rolls-Royce Cullinan pulled up to Cory's Methodist Church on East 105th and Drexel, memories of my past started hitting me like a ton of bricks. The church had a recreation center connected to it, where I would eat breakfast and lunch five days a week during my summer break. Even the staff helped me out from time to time by giving me money for helping around the recreation center and buying me clothes and school supplies, and they became like an extended family to me back then.

That's why when Jennifer offered to hold KJ's funeral at Cory's church, I jumped on the offer because even though I didn't claim a church or religion, I didn't want my son's funeral to be held at a funeral home because we weren't members anywhere.

Jennifer was the recreation center director, and over time she became like a mother figure to me. She treated me like I was her son in so many ways, and she was the mother I always wished I had. She was doing the things my mother should have done, like making sure I ate dinner, helped me with my homework, bought me clothes when she could afford to, and she would even give me a few dollars to put in my pocket whenever she had a couple to spare.

When I turned fifteen, I was old enough to get a summer job. Jennifer made sure my summer-job assignment was always at Cory's Recreation Center every summer. Her team really looked out for me, not because they had to, but because they wanted to, and that's why I blessed each and every one of them once I started making money.

Jenn and I kept in touch over the years, and when I called to tell her about KJ passing, she knew I wasn't a member at any church, so she arranged for the funeral to be held at Cory's church and for her father to preside over the service. Pastor Walls was a mentor to me, and he tried to show me how to be a man. He was the only male figure in my life that was about anything and the only man I would even take advice from. The problem was, the older I got, the less I listened to him because I thought I knew everything when I didn't know shit.

My driver dropped the partition pulling me out of my thoughts. "The funeral director is waiting for the cars that are bringing the rest of your family and the car that's bringing your wife, sir. The cars should be here within the next fifteen minutes, and when they do arrive, the director will escort you into the church to start the service," he said, and after he finished talking, he rolled the partition back up, and I began thinking about how things were going to play out once I stepped outside of the car.

I felt my phone vibrate, and when I looked down to check the message, I saw it was a text message from Sam.

Sam: *Hey, just wanted to give you my condolences, and I'm here if you need me. I just arrived. Do you want me to go inside the church or wait with you until you get ready to walk inside?*

Me: *I'm sitting inside the Rolls-Royce in front of the church by myself. Do you mind coming to sit with me until it's time for me to go in?*

Sam: *OMW!*

Moments later, the driver got out of the car and opened the door, letting Sam climb inside.

"Hey, King," she said before sliding in next to me. Her appearance took my breath away because she looked so fuckin' beautiful. She was wearing a black, knee-length pencil skirt, a red, silk blouse, a black blazer, and some black Valentino heels with the matching purse. I asked everyone to wear something red because that was KJ's favorite color, and her appearance didn't disappoint me at all.

"Hey, you look nice," I said, looking her up and down. Damn, I thought.

"Thanks. You look handsome yourself," she responded.

I already knew I was looking dapper with my all-black Tom Ford suit, red Tom Ford button down, and some all-black Christian Louboutin Oxford shoes. Yes, a nigga was clean as hell. KJ's outfit was an exact replica of mine, except he had on some all-black, spiked red bottom tennis shoes.

Sam grabbed my hand, kissed the back of it, and closed the gap between us. She laid her head on my shoulder, and just that little sign of affection from her calmed me down a lot. Sam's presence and energy had always been able to calm me down and bring peace in my world when it was full of chaos, and that's why we were so good together.

"King, I want to pray for you before everything gets started if that's okay with you?"

"Yeah, that's cool, because I need all the prayer I can get right now," I honestly said, because I didn't know how I was going to make it through the funeral without losing my mind.

We both bowed our heads, and Sam started praying.
"Lord, please give King and Tammy the strength to make it
through today, Lord, because it'll be a test of strength for them
both. Lord, lighten their spirits and their hearts to know that
KJ's in a better place and looking down on them smiling,
because now he's their guardian angel. In Jesus's name we
pray, Amen."

I repeated, "Amen... Thanks, Sam. That was much need-
ed." I reached over and hugged her because she was just what
the doctor ordered.

The funeral director walked over to the car and knocked
on the window, and I rolled it down for him. "Mr. James,
everyone is here, and we're ready to get started." I looked over
at Sam, and my body stiffened, and panic was written all over
my face.

Sam grabbed my face with both hands and pulled it over
to hers and placed the softest kiss on my lips. "King, you can do
this, and if you can't, we're all here to help you through this.
You have to be strong for KJ and Tammy, okay?" I nodded my
head, and she placed another kiss on my lips and opened the
door and attempted to get out of the car. I got confused and
grabbed her arm to pull her back inside the car.

"Sam, close the door please," I ordered. She did as I asked.
"Look, I know you may be uncomfortable, but I want to ask if
y'all walk in here with me, because I can't do this by myself,
and I need you by my side to help me through this, ma. There's
no other person I can think of that I would want by my side
more than you. Your presence alone calms me down and
makes me feel like I can get through anything, and that's what
I need right now."

She thought about what I asked for a second before she
responded, "King, I would love to do that for you, but I don't

think that's best. Regardless of how I feel about your wife, this is her son's home-going service, and I don't want to cause any added stress to either of you. I don't want to have to beat her ass and drag her up out of this church. I will go in ahead of y'all, and then once you're seated, I'll come to sit next to you if you need me to. Just let me know. I won't be too far away. OK?" With that, she placed another soft kiss on my cheek and got out the car.

When the funeral director opened my door, I got out and walked up the stairs and greeted everyone that was standing on the landing. I looked over at Tammy, and she looked terrible. Her weave looked old and dry, her dress needed to be ironed, she didn't have on any makeup, and she looked like she may have lost a few pounds since the last time I saw her. Guilt was eating her ass alive because she knew she treated our son like she wasn't even his mother at times, and if she would have taken him to the hospital, she could have possibly prevented his death.

But regardless of how I felt, she was KJ's mother, so I walked over to her and grabbed her into a hug, and she broke down in my arms, and I ended up breaking down myself. I didn't know how I was going to be able to walk in that church and see my little man lying in a fucking glass box, but I had to do it and say goodbye to my little prince.

The funeral director walked us to the entrance of the chapel, and as I walked down the aisle, my feet got heavier with every step I took toward KJ's casket. When I finally made it to the altar and walked up to the casket by myself, I stared down at my mini-me with so much sadness in my heart I felt like I was about to pass out. He looked like he was asleep and at peace, not dead.

My son shouldn't have died. He should be alive and

running around, playing with toys, and being the sweet boy I was raising him to be. My lil' man, was cheated out of so much —getting married, having kids, becoming president, or whatever the future may have had in store for him.

As the tears cascaded down my face, I kissed him on his forehead, and whispered in his ear, "KJ, I love you. You were the best thing that has ever happened to me, and you'll always live in my heart, son." I gave him another kiss on his forehead and took a seat on the first pew.

Everything after that was a blur for me until the pastor said, "King didn't want just anyone to recite the Lord's Prayer today. He's arranged for someone very special to do it." A soft, kiddie voice blared loudly through the speakers of the church leading us in the Lord's Prayer. Everyone began reciting the words with him.

"Our Father, who art in heaven, hallowed be thy name.
Thy kingdom come. Thy will be done on earth as it is in heaven.
Give us this day our daily bread, and forgive us our trespasses,
as we forgive those who trespass against us,
and lead us not into temptation,
but deliver us from evil. Amen."

Initially, I was able to recite the words, but the more I thought about the words I was saying and his voice, I lost my shit. The recording of KJ reciting the Lord's Prayer started fucking with me and everyone else that was there. The night before he was rushed to the emergency room, I recorded a video of him and I while he recited it when I tucked him into bed. Even though I wasn't big on going to church, his nanny— Amanda—was, so she took KJ to church every Sunday with her, and KJ made praying a big part of his nightly routine. That was something we did together whenever I could make it home before he fell asleep at night. Since he died, I had listened to that recording a million times. So to hear his voice and to see him smiling on the projector and then to look right below it and see that his physical body was still and in a fuckin casket broke my fuckin' heart.

The sounds of cries, whimpers, and wails started to take over the church. It totally slipped my mind that I had added that part into the service, and at that moment, I regretted doing it, but what was killing me was knowing that it would be the last time I would ever be able to touch my son's body and hold him in my arms.

I stood and walked over to his casket and stared down at my little prince, and my heart felt like it was being ripped to shreds, and I started to feel like I couldn't breathe. I felt like I was having an out-of-body experience, and before I knew it, I leaned into the casket and picked KJ's little body up and the church went into an uproar. I put his cold cheek up to mine and rocked his body in my arms back and forth, and it felt like the many times I did it when he was alive, before I tucked him into bed at night. The only difference was his body was cold and hard, and that was the moment I realized my son was gone forever.

I could feel someone lay their hand on my back and start rubbing their hand in a circular motion. My eyes were closed tightly because I just needed that last moment with KJ, and that's when the smell of her perfume invaded my nose pulling me out of the trance like state I was in. I could feel her body lean into mine, and then Sam said, "King, say your goodbyes and lay your son down so he can rest in eternal peace, baby."

Sam continued trying to coax me into laying my son

down, but I just needed a little more time with him. After a couple of minutes, I took Sam's advice, said my last goodbye, kissed him on his forehead, and laid his body back into his casket, tucking him in with his favorite Spiderman blanket and Spiderman action figure. I stared down at him for a few more minutes and turned around and walked back to the pew. Before I could sit down, Sam pulled me into a much-needed hug, and I laid my forehead on her shoulder, and I wept for my son. The crew stood up and surrounded us, and we stood there mourning my son for what seemed like forever, but at that moment, I felt the love from my family and the love that Sam had for me. We had that eternal love... The type of love that regardless of if were apart for ten years, whenever were brought back together, the feelings and emotions rush back immediately for the both of us.

Before KJ was born, I had experienced love but never the unconditional love that a parent has for their child. My heart was made of stone, and I refused to allow love to live there ever again, especially after Sam hurt me when she broke up with me when we were sixteen years old. I was a coldhearted and cutthroat nigga when I was out there in those streets, but when my son came into this world, he gave me something I was never able to get from anyone my entire life. He softened my heart, and I was finally able to experience unconditional love, something I never got from my mother. I prayed KJ's death didn't damage me and turn my heart back into stone. If it did, then love might not have been strong enough to penetrate my cold heart again.

6

MRS. TAMELA JAMES

Tammy

It had been some weeks since we buried KJ, and I person-ally had been missing in action, because I was grieving the loss of my son. Plus, I was dealing with a lot of other personal bullshit. I felt so damn guilty about KJ dying because I should have been a better mother to him. I should have taken him to see his doctor when he first started complaining about his stomach hurting. If I did, maybe my baby would have never died. That's why I've been so depressed because I knew it was a possibility my son would have still been there. I had been praying to God day in and day out that things got better because I was a wreck mentally. I was feeling so much guilt that suicide had crossed my mind quite a few times, but suicide is something I could never do, and plus, I had to strong for KJ.

After the funeral, King totally checked out on me, but what caught me by surprise is how Camille stepped up, and she helped me get through the first couple of days following KJ's death. Camille's actions spoke louder than words when she showed me the type of person she really was. And I was very impressed and indebted to her for how she treated me, because I didn't have anybody who gave a fuck if I lived or died at that point.

How Camille and I argued and fought in the past, her helping me through my grief seemed like something she would never do. But she was the only person that consistently checked on me every couple of days, making sure I was good, and I felt I was indebted to her for that because the chain of events that took place after KJ died humbled my stupid ass down, and it had me questioning the type of person I had turned into after King started making money. And I truly believed God was punishing me for being a terrible mother and how I treated King throughout our marriage.

King had me served with divorce papers, and initially, I was beyond pissed the fuck off, but the more I thought about it, the more I realized King should have filed a long time ago. Plus, I knew for a fact King didn't love me anymore, and that's what pushed me to go ahead and make things official with Chris.

We started going out on dates and posting selfies of us laid up on Snapchat and the Gram, because a relationship wasn't official until it was posted on social media, *right*? We both knew it was going against the grain being together, but the heart wanted what the heart wanted, and Chris is who I wanted to be with. Chris said that King didn't care that we were together, so I decided to follow my man's lead. If he wasn't concerned about receiving backlash from King, neither was I.

For a while, Chris and I were going strong, but shortly after making our relationship public, I found out I was pregnant, and yes it was Chris's baby. We were happy as hell when we found out about the baby. Chris was excited because the baby would be his first kid, and I was excited because I felt like God was giving me another chance to do the mothering thing again, even though I messed up so bad with KJ.

A week after finding out I was pregnant, Chris came over to my house, and he was on one. He was going off about being chastised by Wayne over some bullshit that happened at one of the traps Chris ran. I guess some money and product came up missing, and the finger was being pointed at Chris. Chris wasn't even there when it happened, but because he was in charge, the loss fell on him. When he told me what was going on, I simply asked Chris the million-dollar question; *Did anyone else have access to what was missing, and did he take the stuff?*

Before I could even finish my sentence, he began accusing me of still wanting to be with King and that the whole time we had been together, I was fucking King behind his back, which were lies. Also, I was the reason why everyone was fucking with him and trying to find fault in everything he did. After he finished his rant, I began defending myself. I told him, no it was because somebody took their product and fuckin' money.

Why in the hell did I say that? Before I knew what, was happening, Chris lunged over the dining-room table and slapped the taste out of my mouth. He picked me up by my throat and rammed my body into the wall directly behind me. He was squeezing my throat so tight, cutting off my oxygen, until the point I eventually started seeing silver specks floating in front of me, and I knew I was seconds from passing out. Trying to get out of his grasp, I clawed at whatever I could—his hands, face, and eyes—with my nails, but that didn't do shit but make the beating and his anger get worse.

He kept screaming he knew I still loved King, and I wanted to be with him. He was foaming at the mouth with spit flying everywhere. He looked possessed or something, like a wild fucking animal, and I was scared as hell. I knew he had to be high off something, and it had to be more than just weed or alcohol by the way he was acting. I truly thought I was looking at the devil in human form. Chris lowered my body to the ground, and I was able to stand on my feet, but he never weakened the hold he had on my neck. I started to get weak, and my knees buckled. That's what caused him to finally let go of my neck, which allowed my body to drop to the ground like a rag doll. I immediately began grabbing at my neck and gasping for air, and it felt like I wasn't getting enough oxygen, no matter how hard I tried.

I guess he wasn't satisfied with what he had already done because as I continued to lay on the ground, Chris started kicking me repeatedly in the stomach, ribs, and back. All I could do was scream and hope that the screaming pulled him out of whatever mental episode he was having. *You're going to kill the baby, Chris. Please stop.* It didn't help, and at this point, I had no doubt in my mind that Chris was going to kill me and this baby. His eyes were dark, and it was like he blacked out. Shit, at a certain point, I passed out myself, and when I came to, Chris and I was in the car and he was rushing me to the hospital. I truly thought I was going to die in the backseat of my car because the pain was that unbearable. Plus, I was having the hardest time taking a breath. I kept going in and out of consciousness the entire ride to the hospital until we pulled up in front of the emergency room.

Chris jumped out of the car and grabbed me out of the back seat and carried me into the emergency room screaming for help. It looked just like how that shit look on TV. The emergency-room staff put me on a gurney and then rushed me back to an exam room, where the surgeons determined I needed surgery immediately. My surgery took about four to five hours, and I had internal bleeding from one of the two broken ribs puncturing my right lung. The doctors said it was touch and go during surgery because my heart stopped while I was on the operating table, and they didn't know if I would make it out of surgery alive.

When the hospital staff finally allowed Chris to come back and visit me in the ICU, he acted so concerned, but when he leaned down to kiss my cheek, he also whispered in my ear that I better not tell them who beat my ass, and if I did, he would kill me. Yeah, that bitch was concerned. He was concerned with the twelve taking his black ass to jail. I was so damn scared he would follow through on his threat that I did as he told me to without question, and I kept my mouth shut. Chris stayed within a few feet of me the entire night, and when the detectives came into my hospital room and questioned me about the attack, he refused to leave so I could talk to them privately. They knew Chris did that shit, and the detectives kept mugging his ass while they were there, and they kept asking him the same questions about what happened over and over again. They were trying to catch his ass up in a lie, but that didn't happen, at least not in front of me.

I was in critical condition for about three days in the ICU, and if that wasn't bad enough, my doctor told me she didn't think I could get pregnant again. And if I did manage to get pregnant, the pregnancy wouldn't make it past the fourth week or so. That fucked me up because whatever man I chose to be with, I wanted to be able to give him children. I ended up getting diagnosed with depression, and my doctors put me on a medication called Zoloft. I guess losing two children within a small window of time would do that to anyone. The medicine leveled my mind out, and I felt like it was helping me a lot, so I made it my point to take my medicine every day.

The medicine had me feeling happy, and I started to feel like the weight of the world that was once on my shoulders wasn't as heavy. Also, the suicidal thoughts I was previously having were gone. Yeah, I was still sad at times, but it didn't overwhelm me to the point where I didn't want to live anymore. I was finally starting to feel like myself again, but then Chris walked his ass right back into my life.

Out of the blue, a couple of days ago, someone started laying on my fuckin' doorbell and banging on my front door, scaring the hell out of me. I opened the door without looking out of the peephole, but when I got the door completely opened and realized it was Chris, fear washed all over me. I was frozen in place initially, but then my body started shaking, and I began crying uncontrollably.

When Chris realized what was going on, he started trying to comfort me, rubbing my back, and kissing the top of my head, and it caused me to melt right into his arms. After about five minutes of him just holding me and rocking me in his arms, he apologized and begged for my forgiveness. We sat on the couch for hours talking about our past, our present, and our future.

Chris opened up to me about being bipolar, and I did the same telling him about being diagnosed with depression after losing our baby. We were both on medication and seeing a shrink. After we opened to each other, my love for Chris grew, and I knew he was the man for me. I had to forgive Chris and trust his word that he would never hit me again. I believed he was sorry for putting his hands on me and that he would never do it again.

We decided to start over and do things the right way, which meant I needed to get divorced before we could make things official. Chris gave me twenty-four hours to get King to sign the divorce papers and get them to our attorney. Chris said if I loved him and wanted to be with him, I could make it happen because that was the only thing stopping him from moving in and the two us being a couple. That's why when I woke up the next morning, I decided to just call King and get the papers signed and take them to my attorney so she could file the divorce papers with the courts.

I was holding the phone waiting for King to answer

my call, but the longer it took him to answer the phone, the more anxious I became. The way King had been treating me was so all over the place, so I didn't know if I was going to get nice King or mean King. When the phone rang the fourth time, I thought the voicemail was going to pick up the call, but instead, King answered.

"Yeah?" King uttered, sounding distant and irritated. *Oh, boy. Here he goes with this rude shit,* I thought.

"Hey... um, King, this is Tammy."

"I know who this is. What do you want?" King barked into the phone.

Now I knew King was still mad, but damn he had no compassion at all for me, and it was always evident in his tone of voice. I started to think it might have been a big mistake calling him, but if I wanted a relationship with Chris, I had to get him to sign the divorce papers. *Maybe I should just let the attorneys handle things,* I thought, but that would take too long, and Chris gave me twenty-four hours. He would move on in a heartbeat, and I felt that was my last chance of love and would never find anybody else to love me.

"You know what? That's OK. I'll just have my lawyer contact yours. It was a big mistake calling you," I said, and I was about to hang up the phone, but I heard him scream my name.

"Tammy! Tammy, don't hang up the phone. Now. What. Do. You. Want?" King angrily asked.

"King, I want to know if you can come over to the house so we can discuss me signing the divorce papers I was served?" I said barely above a whisper because I feared what he would say.

"Tammy, what do we have to discuss? Whatever questions you need to be answered, your attorney knows how to get in touch with mine. Can you just sign the fuckin' papers so we can get this shit over and done with?"

"King, if you come over and discuss a few things pertaining to the divorce, I will sign the papers right in front of you, and then you can go to the courthouse and file the paperwork yourself." I knew that would get him here because he wanted this divorce more than he wanted anything else in the world. Initially, I was going to have my attorney file them, but King wasn't going to go for that shit.

"OK, I'll be there in an hour, and don't be playin' no muthafuckin' games, Tammy, because I'm not in the mood for no bullshit today!" King's voice boomed through the phone, and then he hung up the phone in my face without giving me a chance to respond.

I immediately jumped up and ran upstairs to take a shower and find some clothes to throw on. I grabbed some red boy shorts and the matching red-and-white shirt made by Pink. I grabbed me some red-laced Victoria's Secret thongs, and I decided not to even waste my time putting on a bra because I never wore one when I was at home anyway.

I went into the bathroom and cut the shower on so it could get steaming hot just like I liked it. As I undressed in front of the mirror, my eyes landed on the long ass scar that snaked down the middle of my stomach, past my belly button. Tears ran down my face because the scar brought back memories of being attacked.

Looking at the scar on my body, you would have never known my skin was once scar and blemish free, but that was a thing of the past because that once blemish-free skin was replaced with an ugly, thick ass scar down the middle of my stomach that recently developed a keloid. My hands trembled as I began tracing the outline of the scar with my right index finger, and the tears ran down my cheeks and landed on my breast. Memories was going to make forgiving Chris very hard, but I hoped I would eventually be able to get past all the physical and emotional damage he had caused me.

As the steam from the hot water filled the bathroom, I checked the water's temperature and climbed in. The water was nice and hot as I started to wash my body twice over with my Ivory body wash, and loofah I had hanging from the showerhead. Once I finished my shower, I got out and dried my body off and then sat on the edge of my bed and grabbed the Gucci Blossom lotion out of the Saks Fifth bag and oiled my body from head to toe. Then I grabbed the matching Gucci perfume and sprayed my body with it, and I smelled like heaven. The only reason I bought the perfume was because at KJ's funeral, Sam's corny ass was wearing it, and I overheard King ask her what perfume was she wearing because he liked it.

Once I brushed my twenty-eight-inch sew-in into a ponytail, I headed downstairs to wait for King to arrive, but before I could reach the bottom stair, I heard the doorbell ringing, letting me know King had arrived. As I unlocked the door, my hands started sweating and trembling for some reason, but when I opened the door, King was standing in front of me looking like a muthafuckin' snack. I had to stand there for a second and just take his fine ass in completely, and I felt like a teenager in heat.

I stood there lost in my thoughts as I eye fucked King

because he looked and smelled so fucking good. His Gucci cologne had my pussy purring, and it was fighting with my thong to keep my juices contained. *Damn,* I thought, and he knew he was looking and smelling good, because he had a little grin of his face as he watched me look his body over.

King had on some dark-washed Purple Label Polo jeans, a snug-fitted, burgundy-and-white Purple Label Polo shirt with the matching hat and some burgundy Giuseppe high-top tennis shoes. He had a diamond stud in his right ear, a gold Rolex on his arm, and a gold cross hanging from his neck. He normally didn't wear much jewelry, but I guess he was out there flexing for the hoes.

"Tammy, if you take a picture, it will last longer, since your over there mentally fucking me. Now can I come in, since you invited me over here?" King said with a deep, arrogant ass chuckle. I opened the door wider so he could walk inside, and after he did, I slammed the door shut and followed him into the family room. I noticed him staring at the divorce papers that were sitting on the coffee table with a pen lying next to them. King sat down on the couch, and I went to sit next to him the divorce papers fell on the floor. I bent over and picked up the papers. Suddenly, I heard a loud ass slap noise and felt a burning sensation on my right ass cheek from where King slapped me on my ass hard as hell.

"Fuck, King! Why did you do that!" I yelled. My ass was stinging from him smacking me on it. A smirk graced my face, but he couldn't see it because I was facing away from him. *This nigga still wants my ass. Why he out here playing like he doesn't?* I thought.

"Keep your paws to yourself, negro," I teased with my

face balled up like I was truly offended by him smacking my ass. You know I didn't realize until then how much I truly missed my husband. Just the little slap on the ass had me missing his silly and gentle sides that I hadn't had the chance to see in a while because he had been so angry with me.

"I don't think ole girl would like you smacking my ass, Mr. James." My eyes narrowed looking him dead in his, and what the hell did I do that for? His bedroom eyes were full of lust, and I would be lying if I said I wasn't turned on. I had to pull myself together because I wasn't trying to go there with him, so I knew I had to pull it together, and I had to do it fast.

The problem was I had an angel on one shoulder and the devil on the other, and the devil was thinking, *King, please bend me over this couch and fuck my brains out. Lordt, help me, please!*

"Well, I don't know who 'ole girl' is because I'm not in a relationship." King informed me while wearing a smirk on his face and a devilish look in his eyes. I didn't know what was going on with him, but for some reason, he seemed a little off to me. He wasn't acting like his normal self at all. His attire, his attitude, and the flirting shit he was doing was really throwing me off and turning me on all in one.

That's when the lightbulb went off in my head; King was acting so nice and flirty with me because he was high as a muthafuckin' kite. Normally, King didn't smoke weed during the day while he was out taking care of business because he always wanted to be clear minded whenever he handled KDB business. He would normally wait until he got home, roll him a nice fatty, pour him some Henny, and wind down by sipping and smoking before he went to bed at night.

"So what's up, Tammy? Why did you call me over here?" King questioned me while giving me his full attention.

"Well, King, I had my attorney look over the divorce papers that you had me served with, and I'm ready to sign them so I can move on with my life. The settlement you offered me is fair, and I don't want to drag this out longer than we have to." I was trying my best not to cry, but it was getting harder by the second.

King didn't say anything. He just looked at me curiously, like he didn't believe what I had said. I continued, "I want you to know I do love you, and I'm sorry for all the hurt and pain I've caused you over the years. I know I changed some after we got married, and not for the better, but that's what I saw my mother doing when I was a child. She had me, got married, and ran the fuckin' streets. I didn't know how to be a wife and mother to our son because I was never taught how to be one. That's the main reason I'm trying to change and become the best me I can be." I spoke from the heart because that was how I truly felt.

"If you've changed so much, why would you tell Monique about Chanel and DJ? That situation ain't have shit to do with you, but you stuck your nose in their business starting shit. Now you're sitting here acting like you're Mother Theresa or some shit. You can get the fuck out of here with that bullshit, because you ain't foolin' nobody." King raised a brow like he thought I was lying. That shit hurt my feelings, but it was my own fault he felt that way, so I needed to explain why I told Camille, about DJ and Chanel.

"King, my life has been a living hell since KJ died, and I thought Chanel was my friend, my best fuckin' friend. Everybody turned their backs on me at a time when I needed a friend or my family the most. During the hardest time of my life, Chanel ended our friendship because Damien told her to because he was scared. I was going to put hip his wife on to his secret. So since she turned her back on me, I did the same to her.

"I showed the one person who was standing by my side in my time of grief some loyalty because she earned it. Camille stepped up and helped me when I had nobody, and she's the last person I would have guessed would be there. Camille made sure I ate and bathed, and she even cleaned this house a couple of times. She went above and beyond for me, and I felt like I owed her my loyalty. Your boy got Camille out here looking crazy as hell, and I felt I owed her the truth!" I yelled, full of emotion.

"I understand why you feel the way you do, but I know you, and you did that shit to be vindictive, ma. You can tell that lullaby ass story to someone else. You need to tell the truth and shame the devil," King said through gritted teeth. He was right. I did do it to be vindictive, *initially*.

"Well... you're partially right. Initially, when all this started, I blackmailed Damien. I told him that if he didn't tell you about me cheating with Chris, then I wouldn't tell Camille about him cheating with Chanel and him fathering DJ. But as time progressed, and Camille and I became closer, I began regretting my decision not to tell her. I was smiling in that girl's face, all the while knowing a foul ass secret her husband was keeping from her. Even though she punched me in the nose after I told her about Chanel and DJ, she was still my girl, and I don't regret telling her."

Being over it all and ready for King to leave, I grabbed the pen and signed on the lines marked with for me to sign, and I handed over the divorce papers to King so he could do the same. The look on his face let me know he was confused about what was going on, and I couldn't understand why he was looking like he was so confused. Hell, he was the one who wanted things to be over with us, and he was the one who filed for fuckin' divorce.

I sat the divorce papers and pen down on the coffee table and walked over to the bar and poured myself a drink of Patrón, added two cubes of ice, and poured a little cranberry juice in my glass. I was glad I had set the bar up right before I called King, because I knew I would need liquid courage to go through with signing the divorce papers.

"King, would you like a glass of Henny?" I offered and leaned up against the bar and started sipping on the Patrón that was in my glass.

"Nah, I'm good. Sooo Tam, you still fucking with Chris?" King's messy ass questioned with a smirk on his face, like yeah bitch I knew you were fuckin' the homey.

"Really? I knew your ass knew about us, but you just hadn't said anything to me about it. Is that why you filed for divorce and stopped talking to me?" I wasn't surprised at all he knew about me and Chris, because King always found out everything eventually, and it was making sense why he abandoned me after our son died. "Did Damien tell you about me and Chris, or did someone else tell you?" I questioned.

"Does it really matter how I found out? You're wrong for fuckin' Chris because that's the homie, but to each his own. If you like it, then I love it, ma," King said, shaking his head.

"Well, we've been broken up for a while because he blamed me for whatever problems he was having with you and KDB. A couple weeks ago, we got into a big argument and fight, but recently, we decided to try and make things work." I was being vague because I was so embarrassed, and I didn't know if I could tell King what really happened.

"You're being very vague, so that means your ass hiding some shit. Did he put his hands on you or something during your so-called 'fight'?" King asked, chuckling like it was a joke. When I didn't say anything, King stood up and walked over to me, turned my face, forcing me to look him directly in his eyes. For some reason, I got emotional and started crying. King pulled my body into his and he gave me a much-needed hug, and then he placed his soft lips on my forehead kissing it oh so sensually.

"Come on, ma. Tell me what happened," King asked in a soft but authoritative way, leaving no room for compromising. I decided to just tell him everything that happened between myself and Chris. I even told him that we decided to try and work things out.

"King... Can I ask you something?" King didn't respond at first, and it was like he was in deep thought trying to figure out how he wanted to respond.

"You know you can ask me anything, ma." I loved it

when he called me "ma" because it sounded so sexy rolling off his tongue. I dropped my head and started playing with my hands. King took his pointer finger and placed it under my chin, turning my head so I was facing him.

"Can you tell me why God took our precious little boy away from us? He was the best kid, and he was the only thing we've gotten right in this world, and he was perfect in every way. I've been wracking my brain trying to figure out why... Why would God take something so precious and amazing away from us? Do you think God punishing us for all the fucked-up shit we've done in the past?" I bellowed out to King, hoping he could give me any answer to the question that would make me feel better.

King grabbed the drink out of my hand and placed it on the bar. Then he guided me over to the couch, where he took a seat and then pulled me down onto his lap. He said, "Calm down, ma. You can't blame yourself. It wasn't all on you, because I could have done more or really pushed for you to take KJ to the hospital. I was so fuckin' focused on taking care of KDB business that KJ's well-being became last on my list of things to take care of, so there's enough blame to go around. I thought it was something simple like a stomach bug, but never in a million year did I think he had something that eventually would take him away from us.

"We didn't have a blueprint showing us the best way to raise a kid. Tammy, we did the best we could, considering our parents weren't shit. One thing we can be proud of is that we both did better raising KJ than our parents did raising the both of us. You know don't nobody really know how I really feel about losing KJ but you," he whispered in my ear, and I completely broke down. That was the first time King had ever showed any emotions around me, and he had compassion for me and what I was going through, and it felt damn good. I tilted my head back so I could look up into King's eyes, and it was like I could see up into his fuckin' soul, and that was it for me because I needed him right then and there.

7

KING

When I finally woke up the next morning, I had one of the worst headaches I had ever had in my life, and it hurt so bad I wanted to blow my own fuckin' brains out just to make the pain go away. It felt like I had a drummer beating a drum in my head as I dragged my body out of the bed and walked into the bathroom, grabbing a bottle of Tylenol out of my medicine cabinet. I popped four 500mg extra-strength Tylenol, hoping and praying it helped with the hangover I had from drinking the night before. After all that shit went down at the Hubb with Sam's father, I drove over to the lake off Martin Luther King Jr. Drive. I ended up staying there for about three hours drinking and smoking before I decided to call it a night and go home.

I walked back into my bedroom and laid back down, closing my eyes, hoping sleep took me away from my reality filled with the worse headache of my life. I wasn't going to be able to do shit until my headache simmered down or went away completely. I grabbed my phone and checked the time, and it was only nine in the morning, so I knew I could get a couple more hours of sleep before I had to get dressed and start my day. I prayed right before I drifted back off to sleep that my headache would be gone by the time I woke up.

When my eyes fluttered open, I immediately checked my iPhone for the time, and the clock said it was one in the afternoon, and I thanked God that my headache was finally gone.

I saw a couple missed calls from Tammy and a few of my workers, but whatever they needed couldn't have been urgent because they would have sent a text message containing just the numbers 911. That would have let me know I needed to call them immediately, but they didn't, so I knew it could wait until I was on the move to return their calls.

Tammy's worrisome ass had been calling me for the last couple of days nonstop, but I'd been sending the calls directly to voicemail because at the time I knew I wasn't ready to talk to her just yet. I was still going through the anger stage of the grief process, so I was trying to stay away from Tammy until I calmed down some more. I knew I wasn't ready to have a mature conversation with her, but I decided whenever she called again, I would answer the call and see what the hell she wanted.

I dragged myself out of bed, showered, and got dressed, putting a little bit of effort behind it since I had a meeting scheduled with my chief executive assistant, Dominique, or Dom as I called her, and one of the men that manages our real-estate company. Once I finished getting dressed, I walked over to the wall that had a large black-and-white baby picture of KJ, and I slid the picture to the left, and my safe was revealed. I placed my thumb on the biometric pad. It scanned my finger, and then I put in the access code, and the door to the safe popped open. I picked out a Rolex and a solid-gold cross with a large diamond in the middle of it that KJ got me for Father's Day. Both pieces of jewelry complimented the diamond stud earring I had in my right ear, so I was happy with that.

Normally, Dom and I held our daily meeting in the morning, around nine o'clock, but the night before, she pushed the time back because she had to handle some personal business of her own. I thanked God she did that shit because I was still suffering from effects from that damn hangover from the night before. I grabbed my cell phone off my nightstand and called the front desk so valet could bring my car around. I grabbed my gun and tucked it in the fold of my back and put my wallet in my back pocket. Once I finished my call, I headed toward the elevator, but before I could push the button to send for it, my phone started ringing, and it was Tammy calling again. I contemplated whether I should answer, and by the time I went to accept the call, my phone stopped ringing altogether, but Tammy's relentless ass called right back.

"Yeah?" I answered, sounding dry as hell. I didn't want her to think I was happy about talking to her, because her long-winded ass would never get off the phone.

"Hey... um, King, this is Tammy," she nervously said.

"I know who this is. What do you want?" I replied.

"You know what? That's OK. I'll just have my lawyer contact yours. It was a mistake calling you." She was about to hang up, but I just wanted her to say what she had to so she would stop calling me every damn day.

I called through the phone. "Tammy! Tammy don't hang up the phone. Now. What. Do. You. Want?"

"King, I want to know if you can come over to the house so we can discuss me signing the divorce papers that you had me served with?" Tammy damn near whispered.

"Tammy, what do we have to discuss? Whatever questions you need answered, your attorney can always call my lawyer and get whatever questions you have answered. Can you just sign the fuckin' papers already so we can get this shit over and done with?" I roared through the phone aggravated as hell.

"King, if you come over and we discuss a few things pertaining to the divorce, I will sign the papers right in front of you, and then you can go to the courthouse and file the paperwork yourself." That statement caught my attention, so I agreed and told her I would be there shortly. I knew I was supposed to head to the Hubb for my daily meeting with Dom, but if me stopping by Tammy's for a few minutes would get the divorce papers signed, it was worth the tongue lashing I was going to receive from Dom when I finally made it to the Hubb. But I felt it was time to get things over with, once and for all.

When I pulled up to the house I once shared with Tammy and KJ, sorrow immediately filled my heart. I knew when I walked into that house, my little man wouldn't be running up to me, hugging me, and asking me about my day, like KJ did almost every night. "Fuck, I shouldn't have come over here," I said to myself because I didn't know if I could handle going inside.

I grabbed a blunt I had stashed inside of my ashtray and fired it up. Every time I inhaled and exhaled the weed, the more mellowed out I felt. After the last two pulls, I threw the roach out of the window and stepped out of the car.

Walking onto the porch seemed surreal, and when I rang the doorbell, I was about to turn around and get back into the car, because I didn't know if I could go through reliving the memories I had experienced in that house. Tammy answered the door, looking nice as hell in some red booty shorts and a shirt without a bra, and her nipples were poking through some. I looked her over for a second, and once we made eye contact, lust was written all over her face, so I knew she had been checking me out also.

"If you take a picture, it'll last longer, ma." I threw out there, before sidestepping her and walking into the house. I walked back to the family room and took a seat on the couch. As I looked around the room, I noticed papers sitting on the coffee table, and I assumed they were our divorce papers I had delivered to her. As Tammy walked back into the family room, she knocked the papers off the table, and they went flying to the floor. She bent her ass over right in front of me and picked up the papers.

Slap! echoed throughout the room from me smacking her on the ass with the palm of my hand hard as hell. See, Tammy was on some good bullshit, but so was I, and when she knocked the papers on the floor right in front of me and bent over to pick them up, she called herself teasing me, but little did she know, I was with the shits that evening.

"Fuck, King! Why did you do that!" she squealed, trying to act mad, but I wasn't stupid. "Keep your paws to yourself, negro," she teased with her face balled up like she was upset.

"I don't think ole girl would like you smacking my ass, Mr. James." I guess she was talking about Sam, but I knew that was Tammy being her regular jealous and petty self.

"Well, I don't know who 'ole girl' is, because I'm not in a relationship." I smirked, because it was the truth, and I was barely married to her ass.

"Well, King, I had my attorney look over the divorce papers that you had me served with, and I'm ready to sign them so I can move on with my life. The settlement you offered me is fair, and I don't want to drag this out longer than we have to." I could tell Tammy was upset about the divorce, but truthfully, we were more like roommates in our house more than anything for about a whole year. We hadn't fucked in about nine months or been intimate in anyway, but what I couldn't believe is how easy it was for her to sign the papers. That's why I felt like something was fishy about everything that was going on, and I didn't trust what Tammy was doing.

"I want you to know I do love you, and I'm sorry for all the hurt and pain I've caused you over the years. I know I changed some after we got married, and not for the better, but that's what I saw my mother doing when I was a child. She had me, got married, and ran the fuckin' streets. I didn't know how to be a wife and mother to our son because I was never taught how to be one. That's the main reason I'm trying to change and become the best me I can be."

"If you've changed so much, why would you tell Monique about Chanel and DJ? That situation ain't have shit to do with you, but you stuck your nose in their business starting shit. Now you're sitting here acting like you're Mother Theresa or some shit. You can get the fuck out of here with that bullshit, because you ain't foolin' nobody." She needed to stop all the lying she was doing.

"King, my life has been a living hell since KJ died, and I thought Chanel was my friend, my best fuckin' friend. Everybody turned their backs on me at a time when I needed a friend or my family the most. During the hardest time of my life, Chanel ended our friendship because Damien told her to because he was scared I was going to put his wife on to his secret. Since she turned her back on me, I did the same to her.

"I showed the one person who was standing by my side in my time of grief, some loyalty because she earned it. Camille stepped up and helped me when I had nobody, and she's the last person I would have guessed would be there. Camille made sure I ate and bathed, and she even cleaned this house a couple of times. She went above and beyond for me, and I felt like I owed her my loyalty. Your boy got Camille out here looking crazy as hell, and I felt I owed her the truth!" she yelled full of emotion.

"I understand why you feel the way you do, but I know you, and you did that shit to be vindictive, ma. You can tell that lullaby ass story to someone else. You need to tell the truth and shame the devil," I said through gritted teeth. She had done some vindictive shit that really hurt Damien's marriage, but it wasn't her place to do that.

"Well... you're partially right. Initially, when all this

started, I blackmailed Damien. I told him that if he didn't tell you about me cheating with Chris, then I wouldn't tell Camille about him cheating with Chanel and him fathering DJ. But as time progressed, and Camille and I became closer, I began regretting my decision not to tell her. I was smiling in that girl's face, all the while knowing a foul ass secret her husband was keeping from her. Even though she punched me in the nose after I told her about Chanel and DJ, she was still my girl, and I don't regret telling her." I didn't say anything. I just stared at her in denial ass.

Tammy grabbed the divorce papers, signed them, and then she tried to hand them over to me, but I refused to grab the papers from her, because like I said before, something just seemed off with her. I didn't understand why Tammy was in such a rush to get the papers signed and filed all of a sudden. Now, don't get me wrong, I was all for expediting things, but the shit seemed suspect as hell to me.

Tammy dropped the papers she had signed on the coffee table and walked over to the bar and poured her some Patrón. "King, would you like a glass of Henny?" Tammy offered as she leaned up against the bar and started sipping the drink she had just made.

"Nah, I'm good. Sooo Tam, you still fucking with Chris?" I was smirking because I already knew the answer to the question before I even asked it.

"Really? I knew your ass knew about us, but you just hadn't said anything to me about it. Is that why you filed for divorce and stopped talking to me?" she questioned. She didn't realize when she went behind my back and fucked Chris she ended us, and that was the reason I moved out and filed for divorce, because that shit was beyond disrespectful.

"Did Damien tell you about me and Chris, or did someone else tell you?" she questioned like it really mattered who told me.

"Does it really matter how I found out? You're wrong for fuckin' Chris because that was the homie, but to each his own. Tammy, if you like how you're moving in these streets, then I love it, ma," I responded while shaking my head.

"Well, we've been broken up for a while because he blamed me for whatever problems he was having with you and KDB. A couple weeks ago, we got into a big argument and fight, but recently we decided to try and make things work." Tammy was being vague as hell, and she only did that shit when she was lying or if she didn't want to tell me the entire truth about something.

"You're being very vague right now, so that means your ass hiding some shit. Did he put his hands on you or something during your so-called 'fight'?" I asked, chuckling to myself because it was a joke. When she didn't respond, I didn't say anything. I stood up and walked over to her and turned her face toward mine, forcing her to look me directly in my eyes. For some reason, she got emotional and started crying. I pulled her body into mine and hugged her, and then I gave her kiss on the forehead.

"Come on, ma. Tell me what happened," I asked in a soft but authoritative way, leaving no room for compromising. I wanted her to feel safe enough to tell me what really happened, but when she told me what Chris did to her, I got upset because that shit was foul as hell, but what I wasn't expecting was for Tammy to say she was trying to work things out with Chris's looney-toon ass.

"King... Can I ask you something?"

"You know you can ask me anything, ma."

"Can you tell me why God took our precious little boy away from us? He was the best kid, and he was the only thing we've gotten right, and he was perfect in every way. I've been wracking my brain trying to figure out why. Why would God take something so precious and amazing away from us? Do you think God punishing us for all the fucked-up shit we've done over the years?" Man, I started to feel sorry for her because I realized she was hurting just as much as me.

I grabbed Tammy's drink out of her hand and placed it onto the bar and guided her over to the couch. I took a seat, and then I pulled her onto my lap. I tried to calm her down, "Calm down, ma. You can't blame yourself. It wasn't all on you, because I could have done more or really pushed for you to take KJ to the hospital. I was so fuckin' focused on taking care of KDB business that KJ's well-being became last on my list of things to take care of, so there's enough blame to go around. I thought it was something simple like a stomach bug, but never in a million year did I think he had something that eventually would take him away from us.

"We didn't have a blueprint showing us the best way to raise a kid. Tammy, we did the best we could, considering our parents weren't shit. One thing we can be proud of is that we both did better raising KJ than our parents did raising the both of us." I whispered in her ear, "You know don't nobody really know how I really feel about losing KJ but you?" Tammy's sobs slowed down, and she tilted her head back looking up into my eyes, and it was like I could see into her fuckin' soul.

We just stared into each other's eye for a few minutes until Tammy turned her body around in my lap so she was straddling me. Grabbing the back of my head, she pulled my lips into a kiss, and I enjoyed the softness of her lips. Deepening the kiss some, I took her moist tongue into mine, and our tongues slowly slithered amongst each other. I licked, kissed, sucked, and bit her neck, leaving marks along the way. As I pried her lips open with my thick tongue, I was able to mercilessly invade her mouth, and by that point, we were both horny as hell and ready to get it in.

Tammy unbuckled my jeans and belt, and I felt her hand slither past the hem of my boxers, but I grabbed her wrist tightly, preventing her from being able to push her hand deeper but also preventing her from being able to pull her hand out. A smile graced Tammy's face as she said, "I'm sorry. I forgot... please forgive me." Tammy looked me in the eyes, pleading for my forgiveness that I wasn't willing to give. She didn't deserve for me to answer her with my words, so I took the wrist I was holding and brought it up to my mouth and bit it, and immediately after, I kissed her wrist, where it had started to turn red.

"Sir, can I please touch your big, black, long ass dick?" Hearing her say that caused me to smile on the inside, because even though we hadn't been together in nine months or more, she still remembered how to please me sexually.

"Yes, you can touch it, but take your time with it, and if you don't, you'll be punished properly. Do you understand, T?" Tammy shook her head up and down, but she knew I didn't like that shit.

"Use your fuckin' words!" I barked at her, after I grabbed the bottom of her face and squeezed it.

Immediately, she used the same hand I initially grabbed and put it back down my boxers again in search for my mans, and once she reached it, she wrapped her soft, small hand around it, applying just the right amount of pressure, stroking that big muthafucka in a slow but steady pace, from the tip to the base, over and over again, until precum started oozing out of the tip and running down her hand.

Leaning my head back on the couch, I relished in the feeling of how soft her lips and hand were, as she glided it up and down my rod so easily, and how her lips felt against my chest as she kissed and licked all over it.

Since Tammy was a breast girl, whenever we had sex my foreplay mainly focused on her breasts, and that day was no different. I began rubbing her chest with both hands, squeezing both breasts with my hands. I kissed and sucked her nipples through her shirt, making the T-shirt she was wearing wet from the moisture of my mouth. I moved my hands down to her hardened nipples, and I pinched and sucked in them to the point I knew it was causing her pain, and then I bit each of her nipples through her shirt, causing Tammy's freaky ass to moan out real loud, and I continued with my assault, showing each breast the same amount of attention and pain.

Tammy aggressively started removing my hat and shirt. She was moving so fast she ended up ripping my shirt. "Damn, Tamm. It's like that, ma?" I asked while chuckling. I was surprised because normally I was the aggressor, but Tammy was acting like an animal in heat, so I knew things were about to be interesting.

She began kissing me aggressively on the mouth, sloppily just like I liked it, and I realized we both were starting to lose control. "Aye, Tammy, take your clothes off, or I'm ripping that shit off your body," I demanded I stood to take the rest of my clothes off. She only had a few seconds to obey my order because I needed to get up in her wetness. She stood and did exactly as I asked her to, sexily and slowly. She waited until I was completely naked on purpose, and once I was naked, she began stroking my shit as I maintained eye contact with Tammy the entire time she stripped, intensifying the sexual hunger between the two of us.

When she was about to remove her laced, red panties, I stopped her, and I quickly pulled her body over to me, making sure her pussy came crashing into my opened mouth, which was opened as wide as it would go. As her pussy crashed into my mouth, it covered her entire clit, and I sucked on it through her red-laced panties.

"Oh, shit, daddy," Tammy softly moaned out.

My fingers went in search for the crotch of her panties, and when I struck gold, I realized they were soaking wet. I slid two fingers through the side of her soaking-wet panties, and once I reached her pussy lips, I spread them apart and stuck two fingers inside her canal. It was soaking wet to the point her juices were running down my fingers. I continuously rammed my fingers in and out of her pussy vigorously, and once my middle finger started taping on her G-spot, Tammy started losing control.

"This shit feels good as fuck," Tammy moaned out. I

pulled my fingers out of her and stuck those two fingers into her mouth. Tammy sucked on my fingers while she pinched and pulled on her nipples, and I stroked my dick. I removed my fingers from here mouth and grabbed the sides of the flimsy string on the sides of her panties and ripped them completely off her body, and placed them inside of Tammy's mouth. My mouth began to water anticipating how good she was going to feel once I was up inside of her.

Precum starting dripping on my hand and leg from my hardened dick. If I didn't know any better, I would have thought I bust a nut. Tammy raised her body up and positioned my dick at her opening. She lowered herself down, and I stopped her once she was halfway down so I wouldn't bust quick as hell. Once I was ready, I pushed her all the way down to the base, and my shit was hard as steel, so I knew it was uncomfortable, and her facial expression told me my assumption was correct, but I didn't give a fuck, because she needed to feel some pain. Tammy's pussy was wet and warm, and her walls were tight as hell.

I began lifting her up and down a couple times, but then Tammy took over, rotating her hips in a circle while bouncing up and down on my shit like it was a pogo stick. She wasn't going all the way down though, so I had to help her because she always had a problem taking all ten inches of me. I placed my hands on her ass so I could push her all the way down on my dick, and I made sure her pussy touched the base of my dick.

Tammy spit out her panties and loudly expressed, "Fuck, King! It's too deep, baby... Oh, shit... Oh, shit! Daddy, it's too deep," but her ass didn't stop riding me.

Tammy transitioned into the froggy position, and she was bouncing, winding, and cutting up. "Fuck, this feels good as fuck! That pussy wet as hell for daddy. Pop that shit for a real nigga," I said as I slapped her a couple of times on her ass hard as fuck, which in turn, caused her pussy to get wetter. And I can't lie, she was fuckin' the shit out of me, and if I didn't take control of the situation, I would've nutted within the next couple of seconds.

I wrapped Tammy in my arms and pulled her chest to mine, and I started drilling her from the bottom. I was able to give her all ten inches of me. "Please, King! I'm about to cum... Shit! It's too deep... It's too deep, daddy!" Tammy yelled out like that was going to stop me from drilling her ass or something.

"You better hold that shit because I'm not ready for you to cum yet," I aggressively ordered while tearing her guts up from the bottom. "If you cum, you're going to have to suffer the consequences, ma," I warned while picking up the pace even more.

She started shaking her head from side to side, while screaming, "King, I can't," repeatedly.

"Tammy, you better hold that shit," I ordered as I picked up the pace, slamming harder and harder into her.

"King, I can't!" she screamed out. I stopped fucking her from the bottom and told her to stand up. Her legs were wobbly as hell, and she almost fell, but I caught her as we changed positions. She positioned her hands flat on the couch—head down, ass up—and I rammed all of me into her from the back, without giving her time to get herself together, and I was tearing her guts up. She was getting punished for fuckin' with Chris's weak ass and for whatever else I could think of at the moment. She kept complaining I was too deep, but after four extremely-aggressive pumps, she came, and her juices started squirting all over my dick like Niagara Falls. It was running all down her legs onto the floor. My ignorant ass kept thumping her G-spot so she could squirt for a minute.

"Fuckkk! This shit juicy as fuck, ma! You hear her talkin' to me," I teased, because all I could hear in the room was Tammy's pussy making farting and slushy sounds. It was so wet from her squirting everywhere.

"Ah, King, you too deep!" She began trying to push on my thighs so I wouldn't go so deep, but I slapped her hands away and continued with my assault. I pulled both of her hands behind her back and locked them in place in the small of back, and I pushed her face further into the couch, and I started digging for gold, going even deeper.

"Oh, my God, King! You're too deep, baby! I'm about to cum again. I'm about to... cum!"

"Let that shit go then, because I am too! Fuck! Your tight ass walls gripping me hard, ma. She keeps trying to push me out, but that ain't happening," I said as I slapped her ass like four times hard as hell, but I didn't slow down my pumps at all.

Tammy began trying to push herself up, but I pushed her head back down into the couch. She cried out, "Wait! Wait, King! Fuck, I can't. I'm cumminnnn'!" Tammy's body was shaking like she was having a seizure, and I had to hold her up so she wouldn't fall onto the couch, because the position she was in had my nut rising.

Within seconds, I followed behind her and came

myself, but I pulled out right before my nut started to shoot out and squirted it on her ass. I had a strong pull-out game. "Fuckkkk," I grunted while I milked all my kids on her ass. Then I let her go, and she fell down on the couch.

I stood there for a couple of minutes trying to get my mind right, and then I looked around for something I could use to wipe my dick off with. I cleaned my dick off with some Kleenex she had on the coffee table, and then I plopped down on the couch next to her.

"Damn, you beat this pussy up. Damn, King, you couldn't wipe me off?" I looked at her like she was crazy, so Tammy grabbed some tissues and wiped herself off, and then she threw the tissues on her clothes, so I did the same—threw the tissue on top of her clothes. Tammy slowly crawled over to me and laid her head on my chest trying to catch her breath. I slowly pushed her off of me, stood, and grabbed my clothes, headed for the bathroom.

"Aye, I'm about to clean myself up real quick," I informed Tammy and headed toward the downstairs bathroom where I washed up, and once I finished, I walked out of the downstairs bathroom, and Tammy was laying in the same spot, naked and sleep. *I put that bitch in a coma with my dope dick,* I thought.

"You're about to leave?" Tammy asked, looking surprised.

"Yeah, I got some moves I gotta make."

The longer I stood there looking at Tammy, the angrier I got thinking about all the bullshit that nigga Chris had been able to do right under my nose, but what I truly didn't understand is why he was even doing the bullshit at all?

"Aye, I got a question for you. Do you know where Chris been hiding out at? If you do, I need you to run me that address. He stole some product and money from me, and I'm killing that nigga on sight whenever I catch up with him." I looked down into Tammy's eyes because I could always tell if she lied to me because she had a tell.

"No. The last time we talked, he said I had to get you to sign the divorce papers and have one of our attorneys file it with the courts before we could get back together. That was days ago, and I haven't talked to him since," Tammy vocalized, and I could tell she wasn't telling the truth, but what I didn't understand is why she was even considering getting back with Chris's looney-toon ass after what he did to her and their child.

"Is that why you called me over here today? Because of him?" I questioned her with a look of disgust written all over my face.

She didn't answer me right away, and that let me know how weak she really was. "Yes," she hesitantly answered.

"You know what it is, Tammy. Y'all can spend the rest of your lives together. Aye, come walk me out real quick." I turned and walked out of the family room toward the front door.

"King, hold up. Let me throw on some clothes real quick." I forgot she didn't have on any clothes, but it really didn't matter to me at that point. I pulled my nine from the small in my back, and l screwed the silencer on it and put one in the chamber. I couldn't believe I was about to do what I was about to do, but it was something that had to be done.

I closed my eyes for a second, and when I heard

Tammy moving around in the family room, I opened my eyes, positioned myself in a shooting stance, and waited for that bitch to turn the corner. When she turned the corner, I popped her ass—one in the head and two to the heart. Her body dropped to the ground, and as I walked over to Tammy's dead corpse, the adrenaline started coursing through my body, and it made me feel like I was having an out-of-body experience. It took a few minutes for me to shake it off, but when I did, I looked down at her body, and I didn't have an ounce of remorse.

I yelled at her dead corpse, "Yeah, bitch! That's for KJ!"

I pulled out my burner and called cleanup, so they could come and remove her body and clean up all the blood and brain matter that flew all on the walls and the floor.

"Hey, I need one pizza delivered with everything on it," I said into the phone. I hung up and sent them the address. The one pizza meant I needed them to get rid of one body, and everything on it meant I needed them to clean multiple surfaces. I swear I didn't plan on killing my wife, even though everyone wanted me to, but when she lied to my face, I knew it was time for that bitch to go.

See, ever since KJ died, I had been feeling off, and I just didn't feel like myself. I called Bennie up and told him how I was feeling—the rage and my sexual appetite increased, plus a few other things. He told me to head over to the emergency room because he was still at work. He checked me out, drew some blood from me, and they found out that I had or still was being drugged, but at the time, they couldn't tell exactly what drug was used. He had to send the sample to another lab so they could determine the drug Chris used.

Another side effect from the drug was liver failure, and my test results showed I was at the beginning stages of liver failure. So either the liver failure was going to get better and go away, or I would eventually go into complete liver failure and need a liver transplant. Bennie started me on a medication to hopefully stop any more damage from happening, and that was all we could do until I had a liver biopsy done.

That drug had me acting a fuckin' fool, and that was the reason I choked my beautiful Sammie and fought Bennie that night. The drug had me in a state where I wasn't thinking clearly and hallucinating and shit. That was the reason Bennie wasn't really fighting me back or why he didn't just pop my ass when I choked Sam. He knew I was fucked up. Believe me when I say that Bennie could have gotten out of that chokehold I had him in. The reason he didn't was because he would have had to hurt me badly to get out of the chokehold.

See, I didn't know how involved Tammy was with the shit Chris had been doing to me and the crew, but her dumb ass gave Chris access to me. I didn't know how Chris got it, but he used the keycard I gave her to get into my condo downtown, where I had been staying since I left Tammy. And when we pulled the security footage, it showed him putting something inside of the protein mix I used every morning for my protein shakes.

Keys also pulled Tammy's phone records and text message threads, and she had a lot of text messages from Chris with him asking Tammy to help him set me up. In Tammy's defense though, Keys did say Tammy refused to help him every time he asked her, but I couldn't take any chances with my life.

That drug may have costed me the last chance I had to be with Sam. I loved Sam, and she was the only woman I ever loved, but I broke a promise I made to Sam by putting my hands on her. I hadn't talked to her about it, because I was so embarrassed, and I didn't want to hear her say she didn't forgive me. After I handled a couple of other things, I was going to slide over to Sam's and apologize for what I did and explain to her what caused me to act that way. I planned on asking her for her forgiveness, and I prayed she would forgive me so we could move on.

8

MR. DAMIEN WASHINGTON

Damien

It had already been a rough couple of weeks when Romello and I went to New York for five days to meet with our new connect, Carter. The deal we were putting together would take the weaponry aspect of the business to a whole 'nother level. Since it was our first time working with Carter and his team, he wanted to meet all three of the leaders of KDB, but once I explained to him all the shit we had going on and what happened to KJ, he understood. Plus, Bennie had to hold things down by himself while I was in New York, so he agreed to meet with just me. Carter had also required for me to fly out to New York for the meeting so we could meet in person and so I could see how his operation worked. I can't lie, he had a nice little setup, so it wasn't hard for us to come to an agreement that benefited us both, and we both made a lot of gotdamn money.

Once we finalized the deal, Carter decided to show us how he treated his people, so he treated us a night on the town while we were in NYC. He took us to a restaurant called Eleven Madison Park for dinner, and that was a new experience for me and Romello. We dressed and played the part, but we were some hood niggas at heart, so that boujee shit wasn't our thing.

After we ate dinner, Carter took me and Romello to the 40/40 Club and got us "white-boy wasted". It was bitches everywhere tempting the hell out of me, and I tried to be on my best behavior, but them hoes was relentless, and I didn't stand a chance against them new breed of young bitches because them hoes just don't give a fuck. They're a little different than the girls in Cleveland.

King Carter was the man, and when we walked in the club with him, it was like we walked in with a mutha-fuckin' celebrity because that's how everyone treated us. The first thing we did was go to the VIP room he reserved. Carter had everything setup like it was a strip club, and I was excited as hell. I had died and gone to heaven.

Every table had top-shelf liquor setups on them and an array of drugs—weed, cocaine, etc. I stayed to what I knew was true, and that was liquor, and when I sat down, Carter handed me a bottle of Pure White Hennessy, and yes, I was impressed with how he treated his people. I was a big weed smoker, and the shit they were smoking was some heat, but a nigga had trust issues, and I refused to end up walking around looking like fuckin' Pookie crackhead ass because someone laced my weed. I didn't give a fuck whose feelings I hurt, but I only smoked my own shit, regardless of where I was or who I was with.

Carter hired about ten bad ass strippers that he had scattered throughout the room. Two to each booth, and it was stacks of ones on each table for us to tip the dancers with while they stripped. I swear on my kids' lives that I tried not to fuck one of them broads, but it was this one stripper in particular who reminded me of my chocolate drop, Camille, and I was like putty in her hands. It was something about a chocolate woman with smooth skin without any marks on their badass body.

Before I knew it, she pulled my dick out and started sucking the nut up out of that muthafucka, and I let her do her thang, but her giving me some bomb ass neck was as far as I was going to allow it go. She ended up swallowing all my kids, not letting a single drop get away. Luckily, it was only me and Romello in the booth, but the booth wasn't hidden, so if you looked our way, you could see ole girl doing her thang. I could tell Carter's team did that shit on a regular basis because they weren't fazed one bit when she pulled my shit out and necked it.

After about two hours, we went to the main floor and kicked with the common folk for a while, and I ended up enjoying myself even more. I felt at home with them New York niggas. Romello's dumb ass acted a plum ass fool. He was wildin', but he was living his best life, and when we left the 40/40 Club, Mello had two baddies walking out with us when we headed back to our hotel. They were going back to his room to have a threesome. He asked me if I wanted to join them, but I passed because I already felt like shit for letting Chocolate Thunder, suck me off in the private room. Plus, I missed my wife, and I was thinking about breaking a rule I put into place and call her to check on her and the kids. I was happy for Romello though, because he was single and livin' life in New York.

Romello and I was trippin' because we'd never been envied by men and wanted by women like we were that day. Yeah, we had clout in Cleveland, but that was some next-level shit, but I knew eventually, KDB would be on Carter's level if things played out right, which I was quite sure they were.

The next morning, we missed our flight, so we ended up taking a red-eye, and I was pissed because I missed my kids, and I wanted to see all three of my girls before they called it a night. As Romello and I walked through Cleveland Hopkins Airport, we saw a bar, and I wanted to stop and get me a nightcap before I went home.

"Aye, Mello, let's stop at this bar and throw back a few while we're waiting on Main slow ass to pick us up." He was down, so we decided to take a seat at a table in Bar Symon's and ordered two shots of Patrón and two Heineken beers.

"Have you talked to Camille at all since we left Friday?" Mello asked.

"Nah, you know we turn our phones off until we touch back down in Cleveland. I'm going to call her once we get into the car. I just need a few more minutes before I cut my phone on and deal with the bullshit that's in my life."

"So you still haven't told her about DJ I assume?"

"Your assumption is correct, and I'm not going to tell her shit. I'm going to wait it out until she finds out because I'm sure Tammy should be telling her real soon. Chanel's nagging ass been getting on my fuckin' nerves lately. She wants me to leave Camille and my kids so I can be with her and DJ, and she's slow as hell if she thinks that's even an option. Me and Camille's shit is 'til the casket drops, my nigga, 'til death do us part. Shit, I'll never leave Camille. She'll have to quit fuckin' with me, and even then, I probably ain't goin' nowhere, and I'm killing every nigga that even looks in her fuckin' direction. I'm lurking in the bushes and all that shit." Mello and I started laughing because the shit was funny but also because we both knew I was speaking facts.

Just that quick, I decided I wasn't telling my wife shit. I was thinking about telling her, but during the conversation I was having with Romello, it made me realize I'm not sane enough to see Camille with another nigga because I love her black ass too much. Fuck that! Divorce is off the table. She couldn't be with another nigga, and she definitely couldn't bring another nigga around my kids.

"D, Main slow ass just sent me a text saying he's ten minutes out, but you know that really means he's fifteen to twenty minutes away. I just want to say I had a mutha-fuckin' ball in New York, and if you ever have to go again, I'm your man. What we did last night goes down in the history book." We both dapped hands because that nigga wasn't lying.

We finished our drinks and headed toward the designated pick-up location outside of the airport. Once we realized Main still hadn't arrived, I pulled out my cell phone, cut it on, and waited for all the messages to pour in. My phone sounded like a damn slot machine with all the text message alerts that came through from Chanel, and surprisingly, I only had one from my wife. I decided to call Chanel first since she sent so many texts stating *call ASAP*, and *important*. I hoped everything was alright with DJ because she knew I was out of town, so she normally wouldn't waste her time texting or calling, knowing I wouldn't receive the messages until I touched back down, so I became a little concerned.

I dialed her number and waited for her to answer, which she answered on the first ring. "Hello?" she hurriedly answered, sounding upset about something.

"What's good, ma? Why the fuck you text me so many times?" I questioned.

At first, she didn't say anything, but she whispered out, "Dame, she knows."

"Why in the hell are you whispering, and who knows, and what do they fuckin' know?" Before the words finished crossing my lips, it registered what the fuck she was talking about. Now I knew why I had an eerie feeling ever since I stepped off the plane.

"I'm whispering because I don't want the people around me to hear what I'm saying, and Camille knows about us sleeping together. Tammy said she took her out for lunch and told her, and she said Camille punched her in the nose, almost breaking it, and then she stormed out." My words got caught in my throat, and I didn't even know what to say.

I eventually bounced back and asked, "Okay... so she told her about us, but did she say anything about DJ?" The line went silent, and I thought maybe she hung up or something. I looked at my screen on my phone to make sure the call was still connected, which it was. "Chanel, I know you fuckin' heard me!" I yelled through the phone louder than I wanted, but I wish a nigga would have said something. People that were standing around us jumped and started moving away from where we were standing like some pussies. But didn't nobody say shit.

"Yeah... She told Camille about DJ." The situation was so fucked up, and I really didn't want to deal with that shit right then, but I had no choice.

"Fuckkk!" I yelled through the phone, pissed the fuck off because if what Chanel had told me was true, all hell was about to break loose. I fucked up so many times before, but I'd never brought a kid home, and I believed that's why Camille was able to overlook my cheating in the past. But to bring a baby home is some totally different shit. I didn't think she was going to be able to forgive me, and I already knew she wasn't going to accept my son. Honestly, the situation wasn't fair to neither Camille nor DJ, but he was truly the innocent one that would be affected the most. "Let me call you back, Chanel," I responded through gritted teeth. I didn't even wait for her to respond before I clicked her off my line. I went to my text messages to read the message Camille sent me and realized it was a long ass book she sent Friday night—the day I left.

Camille: I didn't want to do this like this, but I'm drunk and pissed, so it is what it is. I never thought you could find a way to hurt me worse than you have in the past, but I give you a standing ovation because you did it. I know you back fucking with Chanel, and please don't deny it. I knew something's been off for a while, but I didn't have the courage to look for shit because I knew the hurt would be too much. I made myself very clear the last time you cheated that we were over if it happened again. I almost went to jail behind that hoe Chanel and your community-dick having ass. If you're going to cheat, it could at least be a bitch on my level or higher, but nooooo, your weak ass downgrades. You go snag the same gutter rat that has been trying to break our marriage up for years. You, Bennie, and King begged me to take your black ass back the last time, and I did because of the love I had for my brothers and our family. I didn't want to split our family up, but you can thank yourself for that. I'm done with your ass and this discussion. I have to live with the part I've played in this, but I learned from my mistakes. The next nigga will treat me how I'm supposed to be treated. I hope it was worth it, Damien, because you've lost your family, and I'm filing for divorce. Don't bring your ass back to my house. All intruders will be shot, bitch!

P.S. Oh yeah, tell that bitch it's on sight! -Wifey

What in the fuck am I supposed to do now? I thought. I really needed to go home and try and fix shit because it had already been five days, and she had been sitting on the info, letting it marinate. I knew if I went home, Camille was going to try and kill me, *real talk*, so I didn't know what the best move at that point would be. I let out a frustrated sigh because I hadn't been in Cleveland an hour, and I was already being served a whole lot of bull-shit on a shiny platter.

Main's ass finally pulled up forty-five minutes later than he was supposed to originally pick us up, smiling and shit. I wanted to punch him in his face because he was so happy. We loaded our luggage in the trunk and jumped in his truck, and he pulled off into traffic. Rome couldn't wait to ask, "So what the fuck is going on, D?"

I blew out a breath and answered, "That bitch Tammy

told Camille about me cheating with Chanel again and... about DJ." I rubbed my temples with my middle fingers in a circular motion because I felt a migraine coming on.

"Who the fuck is DJ?" Main asked, looking back and forth between me and the road. Main was cool and all, but I was two steps from shooting somebody in the head, and he was going to be the first on that list if he didn't shut the fuck up.

"Nosy ass... DJ's my son I have with Chanel."

"Ohhh." Main dragged out.

"Nigga, let us pray! In the name of the Father, Son, and Holy Ghost, Lord, I come to you and ask can you have Camille make his death quick, and she doesn't keep him alive torturing the fuck out of him for days? Amen." Romello's bitch ass laughed like that shit he had just said was funny. "Nah, but for real, Dame... you stupid as fuck! How the fuck you let Chanel catch you slippin' like that and drop your seeds in that hoe? When you got that hoe pregnant, you may as well had signed your own death certificate, and Camille's the fuckin' executioner.'" Romello said with a serious ass look on his face while shaking his head side to side. "You know the number-one cardinal rule in cheating is to never bring a baby home, *never*! You're fucked, my nigga! She's going to file for divorce after she skins you alive, bruh, and I don't blame her either."

My anger got the best of me, and I bellowed out, "Nigga, fuck you! Don't you think I know all of that? I've been wracking my brain trying to figure out a way to keep her from finding out or leaving me if she did find out, but at this point, I'm a dead man walking. Man, I was so desperate. I've been droppin' my seed in Camille trying to get her ass pregnant, but that shit ain't even working." I started punching the dashboard while screaming, "Fuckkk, man! I can't lose my wife! Man, I won't be shit without my rib and my kids."

"Cousin... cousin... I can't do shit but keep it real with you. You should have thought about that before you started back fucking with Chanel, because Camille might have been able to forgive this because it happened in the past, and she already forgave you for cheating back then, but to start back fuckin' her is like you spitting in Camille's face. Just know if you need somewhere to stay, my door is always open," Romello offered.

"I know I shouldn't have started back fuckin' with her hot ass, but it's just... you know pussy and throat a nigga's weakness, and Chanel knows that. So whenever we're together, my dick somehow always slips in her wet ass mouth, and she knows I have to sample the pussy after that. As a matter of fact, drop me off at Chanel's spot because I'll be damned if I go home. I already know Camille's going to be on her gunplay shit," I said through a chuckle.

"Alright. Oh, yeah, Wayne told me to let y'all know about the meeting tomorrow at five o'clock. Bennie said he's changing up how the lieutenants handle things, so I guess this will be interesting, considering what happened Friday night," Main said with a sarcastic chuckle.

"What happened Friday?" I asked, turning to look toward Main.

"Well, King and Bennie were wildin' the fuck out Friday. They called an emergency meeting that they wanted everybody to attend. They said it was to introduce Beast to everyone because he's been getting met with resistance since he had to step up for King. During the meeting, King pulled two niggas scalps back just because these niggas was talking," Main voiced while shaking his head.

I was in shock because King didn't normally act like that. He was the more reserved one in the bunch, especially when he handled business. "Are you serious right now?" I threw out there.

"Hell yeah, and that ain't the kicker. To show these niggas they weren't playing, they had a nigga lowered from the ceiling naked as the day he was born. He was moving around and shit, reminded me of when Beyoncé did the same thing at one of her concerts or something a couple of years back when they lowered her ass from the ceiling," Main said while laughing hard as fuck to himself.

"Man, Beast beat that niggas ass, King started beating his ass, and then Bennie's sis walks in and unloaded a clip into his body and head. That shit was crazy as *fuck!*" See, niggas always thought I was the wildcard, and that was furthest from the truth. Bennie and King are the type of crazy that was dangerous, because their kill game was official as hell. My shit good too, but they're nicer with their hands.

"Wait, who was the nigga they had hangin' from the ceiling? Was it somebody that owed us money or something?" I questioned Main.

"Hell *no!* It was Beast's fuckin' father, and they showed him no fuckin' mercy. That was some cold ass shit, and I don't think they'll ever have problems out of nobody in the crew ever again, especially my ass. I ain't scared of no man, but what I am is cautious of crazy. If that nigga can kill his father like that, nobody else has a chance in hell to get away with shit. Niggas was scared shirtless when they left the Hubb that night. Then to top it all off, King and Beast got into it because King choked Beast sister out and that shit was bad—"

I cut Main off and surprisingly said, "What!"

"Yeah. We had to break that shit up, but that's something you need to talk to them about. Just know that shit was crazy as hell," Main said with finality.

"Well, have everything been flowing well since Beast went all Hannibal Lector and shit?" Mello questioned, laughing like his corny ass was funny.

Main burst out laughing before saying, "Hell yeah. Shit been flowing very well, and niggas been on their best fuckin' behavior. Since you've been gone, Beast had me covering your traps, and them niggas been acting like fuckin' angels. Ever since the meeting, everybody treating this shit like they are punching the clock—come in, do their work, and then go the fuck home." The rest of the way to Chanel's, we didn't say another word to each other. I was in my head processing what Main told me, plus all the other shit I had going on before he brought me up to speed.

When Main pulled the car into Chanel's driveway and put the car in park, I jumped out and grabbed my luggage out of the trunk. As I walked toward the house, Mello rolled down the window and yelled out, "Aye, Dame, don't forget we gotta stop by Momma's tomorrow and check on her because you know she ain't doing too well." I forgot we said we would go over there and see her. Every time we set a date to stop through, something would always happen, preventing us from doing it.

Romello and I had been trying to develop a relationship with her again because we really ain't fucked with her since she put us both out for her nigga.

"Alright. Pick me up from here in the morning because we got a lot of shit to handle at the Hubb, plus the meeting in Akron."

"I got you. I'll shoot you a text when I'm on my way," Mello said, and with that, I headed into the house.

It was crazy how King and Bennie had to show their natural-born black asses for niggas to get their shit together and handle themselves how they should have been doing from the beginning. It shouldn't have taken for them to take a life and act an ass in front of the crew for them to understand that what we're out here doing ain't a muthafuckin' game. From that point on, everyone needed to move appropriately, or they would be handled accordingly. *Bottom line!*

9

MRS. CAMILLE WASHINGTON

Camille

It had been a couple of days since I found out about my husband having a kid with his side bitch, Chanel. Damien had returned home the day before, but he stayed somewhere else. I truly didn't give a fuck where he stayed, honestly—long as it wasn't where I was laying my head. I was glad he was back in Cleveland so he could spend some time with the kids because they'd been asking me every day when was he was coming home from his business trip the entire time he was in New York.

It was killing me knowing the man that I love had been lying and cheating on me again, after I had forgiven him and given him a million second and third chances. Then to top the shit off, he raw dogged that hoe Chanel and got her pregnant. Now I have to go make sure I ain't got AIDS or some shit because she was real friendly with her pussy. Damn near every nigga on 10-5 with two pennies to rub together had fucked her. For the life of me, I just didn't understand at all, but maybe it wasn't meant for me to understand.

I looked down at my phone again because it was ringing, and I already knew it was Damien, because he had been calling me all day relentlessly since he got back into town the day before. He was determined to get me on the phone, and it was funny to me how Damien could be such a determined young man when he wanted to be, but I wished he would have been *that* determined to be fuckin' faithful to me. Then maybe we wouldn't had been going through all that unnecessary ass drama.

I was trying to build up the courage to call Damien to schedule a time and neutral place we could meet up and discuss how we were going to tell the kids about the divorce and come up with some type of schedule for him to spend time with the kids. I just didn't have the energy to go back and forth with him about the divorce shit, because I was truly over it. I knew the kids missed him, and I knew he was missing the kids. Even though Damien was a terrible ass husband, he was a good ass daddy.

I didn't think anybody believed I would file for divorce because I had threatened to do it so many times before, but when I met up with my attorney, Sarah Anderson, and put down a five-thousand-dollar retainer so she could get started on the divorce process for me, that was some truth for that ass.

During my consultation with Sarah, she asked me a million questions regarding my marriage, my reasons for wanting the divorce, and about every infidelity issue we've had. After I explained all the infidelity issues we had over the years, the woman was looking at me like I was crazy for still being with him. Hell, maybe I was crazy or a little slow for putting up with all of Dame's bullshit over the years. I guess we all can have a little crazy in us when it comes to the heart and love.

Sarah let me know she would be filing the paperwork no later than Friday, and Damien would be served on Monday by the processor if they are able to find him. She also said it would be best for me to figure out a way for him to be at our house so the court processor could possibly deliver the divorce papers to him. I had an idea on how I wanted to get him to the house, but I was going to need some assistance to pull that off.

Sarah was pissed at me because I refused to allow her to try and milk Damien out of a lot of money for alimony and child support. I could give two fucks about what she thought, because she worked for me. She wanted me to give her approval to allow a forensic accountant to go through our financial records to determine the exact amount I was qualified to get from him. I refused to okay that shit because that left the door open for the FEDS or somebody to swoop in and use some shit that was public record to build a case against KDB, and that wasn't going to happen on my watch.

Instead, I came up with a descent amount to ask for monthly to ask for because I already knew Dame would give me whatever I wanted or needed without question. The only reason I asked for alimony and child support to begin with was so I could piss Damien the hell off with his community-dick having ass. He hated for the courts to be in his business period, so it was going to piss him off

that the *man* would be deciding if the amount I asked for is adequate, but if it's not, the judge would order for him to pay more.

My phone started ringing again for the twentieth time, pissing me off. I didn't even have to look at the screen because I already knew it was my trifling ass husband. I decided to go ahead and answer the phone and get it over with. I placed the phone on speaker. "Hello, Damien. How may I help you?" I asked in a calm manner, and he was thrown off because he expected me to be all *Diary of a Mad Black Woman* on his ass whenever I decided to talk to him, especially after that text message I left.

Damien didn't say anything right away, and I was about to hang up until he said, "Baby, I'm calling because I need you to know I'm sorry!" That's all my pitiful, bum ass husband had to say.

"Boo, you can keep that weak shit, because you're not sorry. The only thing you're sorry about is that your ass got caught, *my nigga*. There's no need to even discuss us right now, because that shit's over, and the only reason I answered the phone is so we can set something up for the kids. They miss you, and I know you miss them—" He cut me off before I could finish what I wanted to say.

"What you mean 'we over'? Pssss! You can keep that weak shit. I told you this shit ain't over until the casket drops!" he said with venom leaking from his voice, but I couldn't care less because Damien didn't scare me.

"Well, I'll play the loving wife at your funeral, rolling all around on the floor in front of your casket and everything. Then I'll sleep very well that night knowing I put your black ass there, six feet under, bitch. I refuse to continue allowing you to pull me into your little game. I won't discuss us getting a divorce again with you without our attorney present. If you don't have an attorney, I suggest you get one." I cleared my throat, and then I continued.

"The kids have been missing you and asking about you constantly, and I told them lies to cover up what's really going on between the two of us. I refuse to tell another lie about this, so you need to have a conversation while you're with our kids and explain it to them why you're not going to be living here anymore.

"I think you should come and stay the night with the kids and spend some much-needed time with them. You can stay with them here until they leave for camp Friday, and then you can go to your new home. You need to explain to them why you're not living here anymore and why you won't ever be moving back.

"And God as my witness, if you tell my kids about your snotty-nose ass son—you know what, I'll keep that to myself. The kids are at camp, and they'll be home around five thirty, so you can come over any time after that. I'm giving you a fair warning. Please don't come here before then," I responded.

"What's the point of me telling the kids anything about us divorcing because we ain't? And me coming home to 'spend a night' is stupid as fuck, ma. Look, you know I hate talking over the phone, and I'm about ten minutes away from the house. Let me come through so we can discuss this shit in person?" he asked calmly.

"Let me make myself clear, and you know how I hate to repeat myself. Don't. Bring. Your. Black. Ass. To. My. House. Nigga! I'm not playing this game with you, and

I'm not letting you in. Yeah, bitch, I changed the locks. If you bring your ass here, just know, I have my nine on my right hip—locked, loaded, and ready to *go*, so fuck with it if you want to," I said very calmly through the phone.

"You way too calm for my liking, and that's why I believe your crazy ass would shoot me, but let me make myself clear. I don't do well with threats, Camille, and you know this, ma... I'll be there tonight at six to spend time with my girls. I got a lot of shit to handle before I can head your way for the night." After he said that, he hung up the phone. I placed my phone down and took a couple of deep breaths, but that didn't calm me down, because a minute or two later, the tears started falling by the buckets.

That was the first time I had talked to Damien since I found out his *little secret*—no, fuck that—I mean his *big secret*, and I hate that he even put me in the situation where I had to break up our home because his weak ass didn't have the will power to keep his dick in his pants, and what hurt the most was that our kids were going to be affected by all of this. Our kids were going to be hurt to the core when they found out their parents are getting a divorce. I hated Dame so much, and I didn't think I would ever forgive him for destroying our family.

From that point on, I wanted it to stay about the kids and not about our relationship, but I knew Damien couldn't do that, and he was going to be a smart ass and try to get back in my good graces, but that ship had sailed away. I already knew he was going to be trying to fuck the shit out of me because he thought his dick changed world hunger, but that wasn't happening, and I had something in store for his ass.

I grabbed my phone so I could send Sam a text message.

Me: Hey. Wanted to know if it's cool for me to spend a couple of nights with you and Kass?

Leaving is the only way to keep my weak ass from fucking him and taking him back, so I'm leaving so I'm not even tempted. Damien never really listened to the things I said, so I knew the nigga was going to be pissed when he walked in, and I walked out of the house with my overnight bag.

Sam: Bitch, you know you don't have to ask. I'll be at work until about five or six, so let yourself in with your key or knock because Nina and Kass should be there. Am I keeping your whereabouts a secret?

Me: Yeah, keep it to yourself, boo. I'll be there around 6:30, and I would love to go out and have a drink or two. We can go down to the flats because I don't want to run into anybody we know.

Sam: Sure, why not!

Now all I had to do was find a club or bar for us to go to. I didn't want to run into anybody that claimed KDB, so I decided we should go downtown to the flats. I really didn't go down to the flats to kick it much, but my girl, Mercedes, did. I didn't really fuck with too many females, just Sam and Moe, but Mercedes was cool as hell, and she didn't take no shit—like me—and that's why we got along so well. I knew she knew what was a good spot in the flats to go to so we could have a good time.

Me: Hey. Wanted to know if you know of a good spot in the flats I can go to tonight?

Mercedes: Yeah, but let me call my friend and make sure

it'll be jumping tonight. What time are you trying to go? Maybe I'll meet you down there.

Me: *We're trying to go down there about 10, not trying to be out all night.*

Mercedes: *OK!*

I went up to my room so I could pack me a bag, and when I walked into my bedroom, the smell of my Damien's Polo cologne tried to knock a bitch right back into the hallway. My hard ass broke down and started crying again. I laid down on his side of the bed, grabbed his pillow, and just hugged it as tight as I could. Reality hit me like a ton of bricks, and I didn't know if I was strong enough to go through with the divorce, even though I knew it was the right thing for me to do.

I'd been with Damien since I was a teenager, and he was the only man I've ever been with sexually. Damien was my everything. I didn't know if I could live without my husband. Hell, at times I probably loved that man more than I loved myself. If I went through with the divorce, I would have to start all over, and I didn't know if I could do that or if I even wanted to.

∾

"Mommy, wake up! Mommy, wake up!" I heard my daughters, Dani and Alex, screaming, and it pulled me right out of some good ass sleep.

"Mommy, Honey said it's almost time for you to go, so you have to get up and get ready to leave." *Damn, how long have I been asleep?* I thought. I grabbed my cell phone, and it was already five thirty.

"OK, Mommy's babies. Let me go to the bathroom,

and then I need to talk to you guys about something, okay?" I stood up, stretched, and headed for the bathroom to empty my bladder and brush my teeth.

As I walked out of the bathroom, the kids were laying on my bed looking at the TV, falling asleep. I laid down next to them and just took in my daughters' beauty, and I could see features of Damien and myself in them. It tore me up that I was going to cause them so much hurt and pain because I was breaking up our family, but I refused to allow my girls see their father disrespect me by cheating on me and having a baby with a woman while he was married to me.

"Guess what, girls," I said. They hated the "guess what" game, so they both looked at me like I was crazy as hell, and I started cracking up. "Daddy is back from his business trip, and he'll be here shortly to spend some time with you guys." They stood up and started jumping up and down in my bed, screaming,

"Yeahhh!" they yelled at the same time.

"Finally! I thought Daddy was never coming home," Alex excitedly said.

"I can't wait! What time will Daddy be coming home?" Dani asked.

I answered, "He told me he'll be here in about a half an hour."

"Can we ask Honey to help us make Daddy some cookies? Pleaseee, Mom?" I nodded my head, letting Dani know it was okay. They both jumped up and ran out of the room, headed for the kitchen. After they were gone for about five minutes, I reached inside the hidden compartment in my headboard and grabbed my gun and placed it in the small of my back. *If you stay ready you ain't gotta get ready* was my motto. I knew Damien was going to be on some bullshit. My plan was to be downstairs waiting for him to arrive, and once he did, I was going to walk out of the door, so I went back to packing my bag as fast as I could for the night.

I grabbed two dresses—an all-white, body-con dress that stopped mid-thigh and some six-inch, black-and-white Giuseppe sandals. The other outfit was some high-waisted, dark-denim jeans, a studded-out gold bralette, and some cute, gold stiletto heels and a matching gold clutch. Whichever I decided to wear, I knew for a fact I would be killing the game. I folded and threw my outfits and shoes in my Louis Vuitton duffle bag with some underwear, bras, and my toiletries.

As I zipped my bag, I heard my bedroom door close and it being locked. I didn't even have to turn around because I already knew who the fuck it was. I could smell his cologne. *Fuck,* I said to myself under my breath. I removed my gun and laid it on the bed. If this nigga touched me, I was shooting his ass, and I was going to serve my time with a smile on my fuckin' face.

Damien walked over to the bed and sat on his side, smelling good and looking even better. *I can't stand this nigga,* I thought.

"Where do you think you're about to go? I thought you wanted me to come home," Damien said with a smirk on his face. See? This the shit I was talking about. He thought that all was forgiven, but it was far from that.

I let out an exasperated breath and looked him in his eyes so he could understand what I was about to say, and I prayed he listened to what I tell him. "What we had is over with, and we're getting a divorce. If you paid attention to what I said, you would know I said for you to come to spend time with your *kids*, not me. I'm leaving and allowing you alone time with the girls because I don't want our beautiful daughters to be affected by how I feel about you. I will be back Friday after you leave, and I need *you* to explain to them why you're not going to be living here anymore and why we're getting a divorce. Please do not call me unless it has something to do with our kids," I said in a very calm voice. I picked my gun up slowly and looked him dead in his eyes because I was flaming hot on the inside, even though I was calm on the outside.

Damien didn't say or do anything, so I stuffed the gun into my bag and threw the bag over my shoulder, grabbed my purse, and cell phone and headed out of my room, but Dame stopped me before I made it out.

"Wait!" he yelled out as he grabbed my arm, preventing me from being able to make it to the locked door. In that moment, I wished I had kept my fuckin' gun in the small of my back. "So you're serious about us getting divorced? Explain to me why this time so different than any other times? I'll give you time to get over this shit, and then we can fix things like we always do, Camille." I started laughing loud as fuck, and he was looking at me like I was crazy. "Camille, quit fuckin' playin' with me because I ain't said shit funny," his dumb ass uttered.

I suddenly stopped laughing and got serious. "You're retarded as hell! Just me having to tell you why this time is different is letting me know you ain't shit. But I blame myself for your cheating because I played a part in you turning into the monster that is standing in front me by accepting you back the first time you cheated. I should have left your sorry ass back then, but nooo! My stupid ass let you back in. Dummy, the difference is you had a baby with that bitch!" I yelled as the tears started pouring down my face. "In all the years you been out here fucking whoever you wanted, I accepted that shit, but I told you the last time we're done if you cheat again. I guess you said I'm going out with a bang then, because your dumb ass brings home a baby... a fuckin' *son!*"

My knees buckled, and I dropped down to the floor because my whole body felt weak and felt like I was going to pass out. Everything I was carrying I dropped to the floor as I was going down to my knees, and I put my face in my hands and had the hardest cry I'd ever had in my life. I whispered, "You had a son with her, something I've been trying to give you since I had Dani. I almost fucking died trying to give you a son to 'carry on your legacy'! I screamed. "I almost bled to death when I miscarried, and you have the nerve to give her your seed!" I yelled as I watched Damien kneel onto the floor, and as he tried to pull me into his arms, I slapped him across the face. "I fuckin' hate you! I fuckin' hate you!" He didn't say anything. He just pulled me into his arms, and at that point I *really* broke down in my husband's arms.

"Camille... baby... I'm so sorry. Ma, I fucked up, and I fucked up bad, but I love the fuck out of you. I'll do whatever I have to for you to trust me again. Camille, I'm sorry!" I could hear the sincerity in his voice as his voice cracked as he broke down little by little. I think he started to realize how much damage his cheating had caused, and I could see the regret written all over his face, but it was a little too late; the damage had already been done.

"Apologies, begging, gifts, or anything else you do won't make me forgive you for this shit, Damien. Please let me go so I can get up and leave, because I can't do this with you right now." He wouldn't let me go, and the more I fought to get away from him, the tighter he held me.

"Damien, please let me go. Please," I begged, but he didn't move.

So I continued, "You want to know why I forgave you all those other times?"

"Yeah, I want to know."

"I forgave you because I love you, and I know neither of us are perfect, but you did what the average nigga does. You took my kindness and love for my weakness, and that's the problem. There's no way I can truly forgive you, because every time I see you with your son, I'll be reminded of how you cheated on me with his mother, and y'all made him. And I truly believe you're in love with her, because that's the only reason I could see you risking your marriage fucking with her again." Damien didn't respond, but I could feel his tears drop down on my face, and it truly shocked the hell out me.

"Oh my God! You're in love with her, D?"

"Hell no! I just realized how much I've hurt you and how stupid I've been to take you for granted like I have. Camille, you're my rib and I can't lose you because I love you too much!" I looked up into his eyes, and any other time, I would've fell into his arms and told him everything would be alright, but I couldn't this time.

Damien grabbed the sides of my face with both hands and pulled my face into his for a kiss, but I refused to kiss him. He kissed my forehead, my nose, and my lips oh so gently. He tried to kiss me again, and that time I couldn't turn my face because he was preventing me from turning my face. Dame parted my lips with his long, thick ass tongue and invaded my mouth, and once we locked tongues, it was over. We began kissing aggressively, and we both got lost in the moment. We hadn't been that in tune with each other in such a long time, and that's when it happened... I fell under Damien's magical spell, and I knew at that point we were going to have sex regardless of my mind telling me *no*, because my body was telling me *yes*.

I broke the kiss and moaned into his mouth, "Damien, please don't do this." I knew I wasn't strong enough to stop what was about to happen, and I wished he would.

"I love you so much, Camille, and I can't lose you, baby girl," he whispered in my right ear as he kissed and licked my ear and neck. We began kissing again, and I was getting moist between my legs.

Dame put his right hand inside my yoga pants and panties, searching for the entrance to my soul, and once he found it, he spread my lower lips apart, and I felt him slide two fingers inside of me. Once his fingers reached the bottom of my depths, I slowly let out the breath I had been holding since his fingers first entered me.

Damien's fingers had a mind of their own, and he was driving me crazy with how he meticulously manipulated my center with his two fingers, bringing me to my first orgasm. "Baby, I'm about to cum... I'm about to cum, baby... Fuck! I'm cuminnnnnn'," I moaned out as Dame increased the speed of his fingers, heightening the sensation. My body shook uncontrollably for some time, and as I was coming down from my first orgasm, Damien slid his fingers out of me and then he stuck them in his mouth, sucking all my juices off of them.

"Damn, Mill, your pussy juices taste good as hell! I need to taste you, and I need to taste you now! Take these clothes off," he ordered. I guess I wasn't moving fast enough for Damien, because he removed his shirt and pulled mine over my head. I didn't have on a bra, and my nipples immediately hardened once the cool air hit them.

Dame popped my right nipple into his mouth and sucked on it feverishly, while pinching and pulling at my left nipple, and after a couple of minutes, he switched and did the same thing to the left breast, showing it the same amount of attention as he did the right.

"Oh, that feels so good," I moaned out through labored breaths.

My husband gently laid my body on the floor, and it was refreshing to experience him treating my body so gentle. He removed my pants and panties by sliding them down my legs, and once they were off, Damien stared down at my body with so much lust in his eyes.

Rubbing his hand over my breasts he squeezed each breast and then each nipple as he glided across them with his hand. Dame trailed soft kisses down to his final destination as I spread my legs as wide as they would go. Damien began licking my pussy how a cat licks his paws, with long and deliberate licks, and it was driving me crazy... fucking crazy.

"Fuck, Dame! Suck my clit, baby." He obliged, slithering his tongue up and down my clit like a long ass cobra snake. He split my southern lips with two fingers, and my pussy opened up like a blooming flower, and she was ready for the assault his mouth was going to put on her. He stuck two fingers inside of me, moving them at a fast pace in and out of me. I started riding his face, and Damien increased the speed of which he was rubbing my clit with his two fingers. I was losing control as he called for another orgasm to come up, front and center.

"Damn, this shit feels good, baby. Suck on that clit hard, baby." He did, but he kept popping it in and out of his mouth, making a popping sound.

I grabbed and pinched at my nipples hard and rough, and as my hand went to stimulate my clit, Damien slapped my hand away.

"No touching! I got this," Dame spoke into my pussy, causing a vibration to shoot through it, and when he removed his fingers, they were glistening from my essence. "Open your mouth," Damien ordered, and I did as he instructed me to, and when he inserted his fingers into my mouth, I sucked my essence off of them, and I tasted so good, and that shit turned me on even more.

"Fuck! I need you inside of me. Now, Dame." I began unbuckling his pants, and he pulled them and his underwear down, causing his hardened dick to pop out, ready to do damage. Damien took some of the juices from in between my legs and put it on his dick as he started jacking himself getting it to its full potential. Damien had the most beautiful dick. It was a thick, brown, and long, nine-inch dick. At times, I had trouble taking all of nine inches, but other times, I didn't have any problem taking all my husband had to offer.

Dame spread my legs as wide as they would go as he hovered his body over me. He looked down into my eyes like he was searching for something, but I closed my eyes and turned my head as he positioned his dick at my opening, and seconds later, he rammed half of himself inside of me, and my body immediately tensed up.

"Mill, relax that muthafucka so I can get all the way in," Dame demanded, and I relaxed my entire body, submissively. He eased the rest of himself inside of me until he was completely in, and I felt like he had filled me to capacity. He sat there a minute before he began pumping in and out of me, and initially, it was uncomfortable, but then it started to feel amazing.

"Damn, Moe, your shit tight as fuck... That pussy trying to push me out, but I ain't having it... and then you're wet as fuck, ma," he proclaimed in between pumps.

He placed my right leg on top of his right shoulder, which gave him more access because I was slightly turned.

"Ah, shit, Dame." He was deeper than before, and it was hurting, but the more he glided in and out of me, the more pleasurable it became. He started digging for gold and started tapping at my G-spot.

"Yeah, I got this muthafucka purring," Damien said in between pumps, and he wasn't lying.

"Shit, I'm about to cum, D... Fuck! Go harder, baby. Go harder, baby," I begged of my husband, which he obliged and started slamming into me. He leaned down to kiss me, and I got lost in the moment, kissing him back sloppily with tongue and all. I grabbed to back of his head, deepening the kiss, and it was like I had my tongue so far down his throat I knew what he ate for lunch.

"Damn, this pussy good as fuck, ma... Fuck, Camille! I love the fuck out of you," Damien sexily moaned out.

Not missing a beat, he was able to get in the froggy

position, and I had almost died and gone to heaven. This nigga had showed up and was showing out like never before. He had never fucked me like this, *ever*.

Maybe this is how he fucked the bitches he cheated on me with, I thought. In that moment, I began to understand why them hoes acted like that over him. He was fucking the souls out of them, and he was fucking the shit out of me, and my soul was seconds away from making her presence known.

Damien was pumping in and out of me gently, at a steady pace, but then all of a sudden, he picked up the pace, and he was digging deep, slamming his dick inside of me fast and hard. "Camille, I'll kill any nigga who ever try to take my pussy! I'll kill you if you ever give my shit pussy away, Moe... Fuckkk! Moe, do you hear me? Fuckkk, your pussy pullin' my nut out, shit!" Damien sped his pumps up, and it was hurting and feeling good at the same time.

My feelings were hurt because this nigga was handing out dick left and right, having Free Dick Tuesdays and shit. He would want to kill me if I did the same thing to him that he'd done to me. I was fed up, and I had enough of his bullshit so I had to say something.

"Should I kill you and muthafuckin' Chanel ass, because you been breakin' that bitch off probably our entire marriage. Huh? Let me know if I need to put some heat to you and your girl!"

I guessed that pissed him off because he laid on my legs so they were flat against both our chest, and he continued pumping in and out of me really fast and really hard. It was hurting, and I tried to push him off of me, but his crazy ass wasn't budging at all. In a way, I was getting scared because he'd never done no shit like that before, and I had no idea how far he was going to go.

Damien kissed and sucked on my neck and then licked my lips. He began kissing me roughly and sloppily as hell, and he did something he'd never done before. He placed his hand around my neck tightly where it was hard for me to breathe.

When he finally looked into my eyes, his eyes were red, and I saw tears rolling down his face, and that shit broke me. With his hand still around my neck, he leaned down and kissed me roughly, and my orgasm came front and center.

"Oh, God! I'm cumming, Dame. Oh my God, what's happening to me?" I cried out as he continued fucking the life out of me, and it caused me to do something I'd never done before. I started squirting, and I was wetting the both of us up.

"No, Dame. Fuckkkkk!" I yelled out as another orgasm shot through me, and I didn't know what the fuck was going on as the tears started rolling down my face. Damien looked down into my face, and that's when he saw the tears.

Damien began wiping the tears away with his hand, but it was useless because they were replaced with new ones. "Camille, don't give up on me. Pleaseee, baby. I know I fucked up, and I'm sorry for that, but I can't lose you and my kids, Camille... Please don't do this to us... Please," Damien begged as he began making love to my mind and body.

10

DAMIEN

The more my wife screamed out in pleasure, the more visions of her being fucked by another nigga invaded my thoughts, and him bringing her body to heights I'd never experienced with her before played throughout my mind. That's when I zoned out and was on a mission to fuck my wife like she had never been fucked before.

"Oh, God! I'm cumming, Dame. Oh my God, what's happening to me?" Camille cried as I kept stroking the Holy Ghost out of her, and I wasn't taking no prisoners. My pumps were fast and hard, and I was digging for gold in that muthafucka. I was on a mission, and that mission involved me fuckin' the soul out of my wife, and I needed her to do something she had never done before, which was squirt! And that's exactly what she did as I fucked her right through it.

"No, Dame. Fuckkkkk!" Camille yelled out a couple minutes later as an orgasm shot through her body, and when I looked down, Camille had tears rolling down her face, which immediately caused me to lighten up on the sexual assault I was performing on her body. I was fucking her like I fucked these hoes, and Camille wasn't ready for that type of fuckin'.

Normally, Camille was hard, and she walked around like nothing bothered her or hurt her, so to see actual tears made me feel like shit because she wasn't crying from the multiple orgasms she was having, but she was crying because of the mental battle she was having, trying to decide whether she wanted to stay with or not.

I wiped the tears away that fell, but more replaced the ones I had wiped away. I knew in that moment, I needed to make love to my wife and show her the man she fell in love with all those years ago. Mill thought I felt fuckin' changed lives, and she was right in a way, but it wasn't the act of fuckin' that I felt changed lives. It was the act of the connection two people have when they're in the midst of mentally becoming one that I felt changed lives. Yeah, I bet y'all didn't realize how deep a nigga was, but it's a lot of things people assume about me, yet very few get to know the real me.

I started making love to my wife's mind and body. I slowed my strokes down, released her legs I had pinned down, and I began kissing every exposed part of her body I could place my mouth on without interrupting my strokes, dragging my tongue on her skin until I found the next destination of the next area of skin I blessed with another kiss.

"Baby, don't give up on me. Pleaseee, baby... I know I fucked up, and I'm sorry for that, but I can't lose you and my kids, Camille... Please don't do this to us... Please," I begged. "You're my muthafuckin' rib, and if we split, I don't know how I would be able to live in this world without the air in my lungs that you provide. You breathe life into me," I whispered in her ear as I delivered long and deep strokes. Camille didn't say anything, which I expected, but I needed to make sure she heard me.

"Fuckkkk," I growled out louder than I wanted to as I came harder than I'd ever cum before in my life.

After I released my kids deep within my wife's walls, I laid on the floor, holding Camille in my arms, silent without saying a word. I was just happy to have her not fighting to get away from me, even though it was short lived. There was no making what I did with Chanel right, but regardless of what anyone thought, I loved my wife.

After laying on the floor for about ten minutes or so, Camille began pulling away from me, and I truly didn't want to let her go. I felt that could've been the last time I would be able to hold her in that way again. I released Camille's body, and she immediately pulled away from me and put her clothes on and headed for the bedroom door. I could feel my wife, mother to my kids, my best friend, my Bonnie, and the best thing that had ever happened to me walk right out of my life. That shit hurt bad, and I had nobody to blame but myself. I sat on the floor wallowing in my own misery for about ten minutes thinking about all the bullshit I had put my wife through. When I thought of everything over the years and broke it all down in my head, I probably would have killed her ass and the nigga if she'd done a tenth of the shit to me that I did to her.

I got up and went into the bathroom and showered, and as I threw my T-shirt on, the girls ran into my bedroom and tackled me, making me fall to the ground.

"Daddy, we made you a surprise, and it's downstairs

in the TV room. We picked out a movie, and Honey helped us make some popcorn." I already knew what the surprise was because whenever I go out of town, they make me chocolate-chip cookies, and plus, I smelled them the moment I walked into the house. They started jumping and climbing on me like they always did when they saw me after not seeing me for a while.

"So what's my surprise?" I asked as I tickled them.

"Daddy, we can't tell you because then it won't be a surprise," Dani said through laughter.

"Well, what movie did y'all choose, because I don't want to watch shit girly?"

"Daddy, you cursed, and now you owe us a dollar," they both said at the same time, and then they both stuck their hands out so I could put a dollar in them. I reached down and grabbed my jeans off the floor, went into my pocket, and pulled out two bills and put a twenty in each of their hands.

"This should take care of me for the rest of the night. I don't even know why your momma started that shit anyway. I've given them y'all both at least a grand over the last year or so," I complained. I couldn't stop cursing to save my fuckin' life, and they always caught my ass, and I would have to pay up, showing them you had to deal with the consequences if you break the rules. Ain't that some shit? Camille tried to teach the girls something, and it was sinking in, but she was teaching me some shit.

I grabbed Dani and threw her over my right shoulder and began walking out of my room and down the hallway toward the TV room. Her laughing uncontrollably made me and Alex laugh just as loud as her, bringing the girls to tears from laughing so hard.

As we walked into the TV room, I could see my chocolate-chip cookies and a glass of milk with ice on the coffee table, and it put a smile on my face. I took a seat on the extra-long loveseat we had in there, and the girls sat next to me and laid their heads on my chest, one on each side like they always did. Shit like that is what I was going to miss the most. I lived for being a father and spending time with my kids. I was a hard ass nigga when I was out in the streets, but I became a soft ass bitch every time I looked into my girl's eyes seeing so much love and innocence.

I popped a cookie in my mouth and complimented my girls. "These are the best chocolate-chip cookies I've ever had, and Daddy wants to thank you girls for the cookies, milk, and the movie. I hate going out of town on business because I end up missing y'all so much... You both know you're my favorite daughters. Right?" They both started laughing.

"Daddy, we're your only daughters, silly," Dani stated through laughs.

"Actually, we're your only kids, so we have to be your favorites." Alex's smart ass threw out there. How in the hell was I supposed to tell them they have a brother by a woman other than their mother? This shit was going to devastate them—not the brother shit, but their mother and I separating.

"Aye, girls, how was your mother while I was gone?" I asked curiously.

The girls looked at each other, and then they both looked at me with sad faces. "Daddy, she's been sad the last couple of days, but she's been trying to act happy when we're around. Last night, when she thought we were sleeping, she was in the room crying. So I got in the bed with her and slept in your spot, and it made her feel better," Alex said, but she had this sad look on her face like something was bothering her, but she was scared to speak on it. Over the years, I learned to let her be until she was ready to talk about it, and once she was ready to share, she would come to me or her mother and talk to us about whatever was bothering her.

"Daddy, why was Mommy so sad?" Dani asked with the saddest face. "She said it was because she missed you so much since you were gone, but if she missed you so much, why did she leave?" My girls were so smart, and they picked up on everything, as you can see.

I knew if I told them what was really going on between me and their mother, it would've ruined the night, and I wanted to enjoy the night with them and worry about the other shit later.

"Girls, your mother's good. She had a trip planned with her girls. She planned it a long time ago, so that's why she left. She was crying because she *was* sad. She found out some bad news while I was away, but I'm glad you were here to help her since I wasn't, Alex."

They both said, "You're welcome," at the same time. If you didn't know our family, you'd swear my girls were twins because they acted just alike, but they weren't twins. They were actually a couple of years apart.

Camille made sure they were close, didn't fight, and took care of each other when we weren't around. I couldn't lie, my wife was a good ass mother and spouse, and the only problem we ever had in our marriage over the years was my cheating. Everything else was gucci between us. Mill had done so much for me during our relationship, and I owed her more than the bullshit I'd been dishing out to her. I had to figure out a way to make it up to her. She was too good of a woman for me to lose.

Dani had grabbed the remote and cut the lights of and started the movie. We watched two movies together, but by the time the third one finished they were knocked out. I grabbed my phone and looked at the time, and it was a little after nine.

I picked Alex up and headed toward their room to put her in the bed, and I did the same thing with Dani. They're so close that when we bought and started to renovate the house, they said they still wanted to share a room. Camille had the contractors combine their bedrooms together, making one large ass room. If we had allowed it, they would have slept in the same bed also. But Camille wasn't going for that shit, because she said they were too damn old to sleep in the same bed. Once I tucked them in—yeah, my hard ass tucked them in—I stood in their doorway and watched them sleep so peace-fully, thinking about how I didn't want to give that up.

My phone vibrated in my pocket, letting me know someone was calling me on my personal phone. When I looked at the caller screen, I saw Chanel's name floating across the screen. I hadn't talked to her the entire day, so she didn't know I was staying here tonight and not with her. She really thought I was staying with her until I found me a spot or figured some things out. That shit wasn't going to happen. I didn't want her ass to get too comfortable with me staying there. Even if I wasn't staying the night with the kids, I was going to get me a hotel room until the contractors were through with my condo. Like I said before, even if my marriage ended, I wasn't going to be a relationship with Chanel because she was a bona fide hoe.

I closed the girls' door and walked into my bedroom as quickly as I could because I didn't want the ringing to wake either of them up, but as I went to answer the call, the phone hung up. Chanel's worrisome ass called right back, and I answered it on the first ring because my ringer was so loud.

"Ma, what's good?" I questioned Chanel.

"Nothing—Um... I was just calling because DJ wants to know if you plan on coming back tonight because he wants you to put him to bed?" Chanel queried. I laughed to myself because she knew damn well DJ didn't ask her that, but in fact, that was a question she wanted me to answer. I think I would have respected her more if she just came out and asked me when I was coming over instead of lying whenever she opened her fuckin' mouth.

"Nah," I dryly responded.

"Oh, so where are you going to stay? I thought Camille kicked you out?" she asked, sounding like she was smiling while saying it.

"I'm staying at the house—"

I paused because I started thinking about me being a single man, and I didn't have to explain shit to her, but if I didn't, I would have to deal with her calling me a million times that night, so I just told her the truth so her petty ass would get off my back. "I'm spending a couple of nights with my girls, and Camille left until Friday so I can spend some time alone with them, if you must know."

"Oh, so she left you there by yourself with the kids. That sounds like a crock of shit. but whatever," she mumbled.

"Bitch, first off, I don't owe you an explanation because your bird ass ain't and never will be my woman. Second, I've never lied to you because I don't owe you shit because Camille's wifey, and that's the only person feelings I care about. Stay off my line from now on. I'll call you when I'm ready to come see DJ or if I want to pick him up and take him with me. You're the fuckin' reason my family destroyed now, and you want to question me!" I yelled through the phone mad as hell.

"No, nigga, Camille's divorcing you because you can't be faithful to save one of your kid's lives. I'm not married to Camille, you are, so I don't owe that fat bitch shit but my ass to kiss!" Chanel yelled through the phone before she hung up.

I couldn't stand her muthafuckin' ass, and the only time I could really tolerate her ghetto ass was when my dick was down her throat, making her gag. I grabbed my stash of weed out of our headboard and rolled me a fatty. Shit, I had weed stashed all over our house because I never knew when I needed to take a smoke, because me smoking kept me from taking a lot of muthafuckas' lives.

Once I finished rolling, I poured me some Henny in one of the customized glasses sitting on the bar in our bedroom that Camille had bought me a couple of weeks before. The glasses were sweet as hell. They're all glass, with black king chess pieces on two and queen chess pieces on the other two.

I cut the TV on SportsCenter, and that's when it dawned on me that I hadn't talked to Romello for him to check in. I dialed his number from my burner phone, and he picked up on the third ring.

With an attitude, I blurted out, "Nigga, why you didn't

check in? You were supposed to call me hours ago," I asked Romello with an angry undertone to my voice.

"I know, but I got a lead on that nigga Chris, and I wanted to check some shit out before I called you or King."

"What lead are you talking about?" I hadn't heard about a lead, but I did check out early so I could go home and be with my kids.

"This broad I fucked with a while back called me and said she knew where that nigga was laying his head, and she was right. You ain't going to believe where he's been hiding out. That's why we haven't been able to find his ass." Romello chuckled through the phone. I wondered where the nigga had been because we *hadn't* been able to find this nigga for shit, and nobody been talkin'.

See, once we went through the video from the security system that was inside the traps that Chris ran, we found out he had been taking money of the top for a while. We went into his apartment and found a lot of his computer equipment that he had left behind. Keys was having a hard time hacking into his laptops, but once she did, we would be able to see everything he had been doing.

The reason we hadn't realized he was skimming money before then was because he hacked our system and was able to change deposit amounts, preventing us from realizing what he was doing. I ain't going to lie, Chris was a beast with that computer shit, but he fucked with the wrong niggas because the consequences to his actions was the reason everyone he knew and loved was going to die.

I asked, "So where he's been hiding out?"

"Nigga... with Toy ass. When King increased the reward amount, her thirsty ass found out, so she called me to see how she go about getting it. I told her I'll call her tomorrow and for her to send me their location. When she sent me her address, I recognized it was hers, so I slid through just to make sure she wasn't on no bull-shit, and when I looked through the window, this nigga was digging her guts out.

"That bitch is a hoe and a bottom of the barrel one at that. That's why I quit fuckin' with her nasty ass, and when I did fuck her, I strapped up extra tight. She wasn't catching me slippin'. This bitch thought somebody was going to play step daddy to them nappy-headed ass kids of hers. Not me, nigga. You know I can't stand kids, especially ones with nappy hair and a fucked-up-looking face." This nigga busted out laughing because he was serious as fuck. He'd been like that ever since his ex-girl-friend tried to pin a kid on him. My family had some good genes, and when the baby came out looking like a black ass Benjamin Button, everybody knew the baby wasn't his. The DNA test came back 101% that he wasn't the pappy.

"Nigga, you need to let that shit go with Hazel E," I said as we both broke out into laughter because that bitch Latrese looked exactly like Hazel E's manly ass from the show *Love & Hip Hop*.

"Nigga, fuck you and that bitch Latrese. Trying to pin that ugly ass baby on me. When she pushed his ugly ass out, the doctor almost dropped him because his ugly ass scared the shit out of her," his stupid ass said.

"Fuck all that. Did you scoop up Chris's ass?" I asked, and then I anxiously awaited his answer.

"Nope. It was too many people around, so I told her to call me if the nigga leaves, or she won't get the money."

"OK. Make sure somebody on him as well, because I don't want him to slip between our fingers. I'll bring it up in the meeting tomorrow. It's at seven, right?" I asked.

"Yes. The lieutenants will be at the meeting tomorrow as requested, and I'll pick you up in the morning around nine, because we got a lot of shit to handle tomorrow." Romello informed me.

"That's cool. Pick me up from my house, and call me when you're in the car and on your way," I said.

"Oh, Camille let you back in already?" He managed to get out while laughing. This nigga was with the shits.

"Bitch, fuck you. You know she ain't let me come home yet. I'm spending a night with the kids while she's gone until Friday. She said she filed for divorce, and I'll be getting served the divorce papers soon... I feel sorry for whoever tries to deliver them muthafuckas to me, because I'm beating their ass, man or woman. I can't fuck Mill up, so they gotta be a stand-in," I seriously explained.

"Nigga, you're the retarded one. You can't beat niggas asses because you fucked up, cheated, and brought a baby home," this nigga said through laughter. I swear I would have beat his ass if he was in front of me.

"Bitch. Fuck. Your. Punk. Ass!" I screamed through the phone right before I hung it up. It was funny how I was ready to kill a nigga because they called me out on my shit.

My plan was to try and get my wife back, but I decided I wasn't going to fight her on the divorce if that's what she really wanted. But if she gave me any hope that she didn't want the divorce, I was going to dead that divorce shit. I knew her heart was saying the divorce is something she needed, and it was sad because I realized that I had broken her with bringing DJ into the mix, and I didn't think she was ever going to forgive me for what I had done, regardless of what I said or did.

11

SAM

It was crazy how I had things mapped out pertaining to how things would go when I returned to Cleveland, and part of those plans was King and I getting back together. But all that changed the night King laid his hands on me. It totally changed my perception of him. I used to look at him like my knight in shining armor. Only a coward put their hands on a woman, not a real man.

He hadn't even picked up the phone to call or send a text apologizing for what he did to me. The only thing I'd received from him was a bruised and sore neck, and he had flowers delivered to me the last couple of days with a card stating he was sorry. But that shit weak as hell because he should've brought the flowers himself and apologized for what he did. Every time one was delivered, I threw them in the garbage, and until he apologized, I didn't want to see his ass.

Camille spent a couple of nights with me and Kassidy, but since it was Friday, she had to go home and check on things. Wednesday night we were supposed to go out, but that ended up not happening because I had to stay at work an extra couple of hours. One of my patient's health started to decline, and I couldn't leave her and her family until I knew she would be OK.

When I got home, Camille invited Mercedes over to kick it with us. Initially, I was hesitant about allowing Mercedes into our little clique, but once I started talking to her, I realized how cool she was, and her and Camille's personalities were very similar. Cedes ended up bringing her two kids with her, which was cool, because Kassidy and her kids played well together. Plus, they were all so well behaved the entire time. So while the kids played, we ate, drank wine, and talked about the fucked-up shit that was going on in our lives. That girls' night was much needed because we all had been dealing with a lot of bullshit, so being in an atmosphere where we could vent and get some shit off our chest was therapeutic for our souls.

Since it was Friday and I had the day off, I decided to run some errands since Camille had just left to go home.

I took care of my hygiene and threw on some black leggings and the matching lime-green-and-black sports bra that I picked up at the Pink store. I grabbed my lime-green, black, and white Huaraches and threw on a cute little jean jacket. When I looked in my floor-to-ceiling mirror, I was happy with how cute I looked. As I was headed out the door, an alert on my phone went off, letting me know a text message had just come through. Once I got into my car, I decided to go ahead and check the message, but when I realized that Brian sent the message, I immediately caught an attitude.

Brian: Samantha, we need to meet and discuss the divorce, ASAP!

Me: Fuck you! You know my terms. If you contact me again, I'll block your ass. By the way, your daughter is doing fine.

I connected my phone to my Bluetooth and headed toward the Starbucks on Euclid Avenue by University Hospital. It wasn't that far from my house. When I walked into the coffee shop and looked around, the first thing I noticed was a long ass line of people waiting to order coffee. Now normally, I didn't mind waiting, but I woke up on the wrong side of the bed, irritated with life, and I wished I could go back to sleep and wake back up and start this day over.

I heard someone yell, "Sam!" I looked around the room to see who called my name, and when I laid my eyes on Damien, he gestured for me to head his way.

He stood up and hugged me before sitting back down. "Sis, I ordered you a caramel macchiato with coconut milk like you asked me to. I felt like a little bitch ordering it too, so be lucky you're, baby sis." Dame's smart ass pushed my caramel macchiato across the table to me, and when I took the first sip it felt like heaven going down my throat. I know I told him to order the drink for me, but he said he was too manly to order a girly drink like that, so I thought I was going to have to get it myself.

"Thanks, Dame."

"Well, Sam, I wanted to talk to you about Camille. I know you already knew she would be the topic of our conversation today. I know I fucked up bad this time. I'm scared I've lost her forever. I know I sound like a bitch right now, but I don't give a fuck. I don't think I'll be able to live without her and my kids. Our kids are used to living under the same roof with both of us, and it'll kill them if that's taken away from them. Knowing I'm the reason our family is being ripped apart has been a hard pill for me to swallow," Dame said, visibly upset. I felt sorry for him, but he was going through this because he couldn't keep his dick in his pants.

I'm not going to sugarcoat shit to make him feel better. "Dame, how did you let this shit happen? There's no way you should have been fucking around, but if you were, you should have used protection, dude, because you're married. There's no way your side bitch should have gotten pregnant and had a child by you."

"You're right. I shouldn't have been fuckin' her without protection, and I wish I hadn't fucked her at all. I had no clue she was pregnant, let alone had a baby, until she contacted me a while back and told me. There's no way I would have let her have my fuckin' seed, and that's why she kept that shit quiet until she had him."

"Are you sure he's yours?" I seriously questioned because he and Camille could have been going through all of that for no reason.

"I had Bennie do a DNA test, and it came back 99.9% I am the father," Dame said while shaking his head.

"Okay, so explain to me how you and Chanel ended up fucking again?" I just wanted to understand what was going through his head for him to do something so stupid, because it was costing him his marriage.

"Honestly, sis, I was over her house spending time with DJ, and I fell asleep on the couch with DJ laying on my chest, and she woke me up with my dick in her mouth, and we'd been fuckin' ever since. Do you think I'll be able to get Mill to forgive me and take me back?" He looked like a lovesick puppy when he looked me in my eyes and asked me that question. I couldn't answer the question for him because I wasn't sure.

"Wow! Honestly, I don't know. When she was venting to me about what was going on with you guys, she sounded like she was done, but you never know what can happen. Only time can tell... Keeping it real though, you brought all of this shit on yourself. You have a ride-or-die chick as a wife, but that wasn't enough for you. You weren't satisfied until you had the hood's biggest hoe on your team.

"Over the years, you've cheated on her so many times. I don't have enough fingers to keep a tally, and that's just the times that Camille found out about somehow. You're a serial cheater, and your wife was understanding of that and tried to motivate you to quit before you lost her foreva—in Cardi B's voice. You didn't take heed to the warning, so now you're out here looking like a lovesick puppy. I truly believe you guys could've possibly worked things out, but when you brought a child into it, I don't think Camille would ever be able to accept him, which in turn means she can't forgive you for what you did," I said, getting angry thinking about how this shit was affecting my sis.

"Do you know if she already filed for divorce?" he asked me with a glimmer of hope in his eyes. I had to crush his dreams because she had already filed.

"I'm not sure if the paperwork has been filed, but I do know she met with her lawyer Monday to discuss filing for divorce."

"Man, I can't believe I fucked up this bad. I can't even

be mad at Camille for not wanting to forgive me, because if the shoe was on the other foot, I wouldn't be able to forgive her."

"Don't give up hope, brother, because like I said before, you never know what can happen." I tried convincing him that he may have a chance to reconcile, but who are we kidding? She ain't taking his ass back.

"Enough about my bullshit. Have you talked to King recently?" Dame's nosy ass asked.

"No, but for the last couple of days, he's sent me flowers with a card basically saying he's retarded as fuck and to accept his apology. But I just don't know how genuine it is." I smiled thinking about how beautiful the roses were and how all the cards basically said how sorry he was and that he was retarded and asking me to forgive him. Even with me throwing the flowers away, it was nice to get flowers delivered.

"Yeah, he's been moping around the last couple of days. I know for a fact he's sorry for what he did to you, but he just didn't know how to handle what Max said. It was hard for him to hear some shit like that because of everything that happened to KJ, so hearing about you killing his seed fucked him up. I think you both need to sit down and have a conversation and discuss everything, because you're both wrong."

"I know we both had a part to play in it, and we both need to act like adults and have a conversation, but I'm not ready to have that right now. You know me better than most, so you know I would never do some-thing like that if I had an option. My father forced me to have that abortion, to break things off with King and to distance myself from Camille. If I didn't comply with his orders, he threatened to kill King, me, and my moth—"

Before I could finish what, I was saying someone walked up to our table and rudely interrupted me midsentence, clearing his throat.

"I see you moved on pretty fast, so is this the reason you can't answer any of my calls?" Brian said loudly so other patrons around us could hear every word he was saying, embarrassing the hell out of me.

"Sam, who the fuck is this white boy that's interrupting our fucking conversation!" I guess neither Camille nor Bennie never mentioned to Damien that Brian was white. I hoped and prayed Brian didn't get out of pocket because Damien would have beat the hell out of him and not thought twice about shit. Dame wouldn't care it was about a hundred witnesses sitting in Starbucks.

"Damien, I would like for you to meet my soon to be ex-husband, MR. I Ain't Shit!" Brian's stupid ass put his hand out so Damien could shake it, and Dame looked at his hand like it had shit on it. I wanted to laugh so bad, but I knew it would make things worse.

Brian cleared his throat and pulled his hand back embarrassed. "Since I had to go through such extreme measures to find you and talk to you, Damien, can I have a moment alone with my beautiful wife? We have a few things we need to discuss if you don't mind."

"Whatever you have to say to me, you can say it in front of him. Besides, I don't trust being alone with you," I said with finality.

Damien stood up and turned toward Brian, mugging the hell out of him. He crossed his arms across his chest and asked, "Sam, did you leave this muthafucka because he was putting his hands on you?" I could've answered that truthfully or I could've lied, because yes, Brian had put his hands on me before, but that was a story for a later date. I knew if I said yes though, Damien was going to kill him in broad daylight with a whole bunch of witnesses because he's a hothead.

"Playboy, this doesn't have anything to do with you, so chill the fuck out," Brian said, which surprised the hell out of me, because he was trying to boss up, but he chose the wrong nigga to boss up to.

At that point, Damien was so pissed I could see steam coming from his ears. He took a few steps toward Brian, and Brian's scary ass tried stepping back, but the table and chair behind him prevented him from going anywhere.

"I'm going to give you one warning, and that's it. Don't think because we're in a store full of people I won't put a bullet right between your fuckin' eyes, because I will, and then I'll walk out of here as if nothing happened and get away with murdering your ass. So I suggest you say what you need to say and then get the fuck up out of here," Damien said with murder in his eyes.

I cut my eyes at Brian giving him that look like *you don't want these types of problems.* See, I never told Brian anything about the men in my life that live here in Cleveland, so he didn't know niggas in Cleveland were a different breed, and they don't fuck around.

"Well, Sam, I came here to see if we can work something out and get the divorce finalized, but you got to compromise some. I know you're ready, just like I am, to get this divorce shit over with so we both can move on with our lives. Don't you want that too, Sam?" Brian asked me almost in a begging manner. It was crazy how when he was broke and didn't have shit, me and Kassidy was good enough for him, but once he started to excel in his career and get a comma or two in his bank account, his white ass was too good for us. He thought he could kick me and Kassidy to the curb so he could marry and have a baby with his white girlfriend without any consequences to his actions. He had me so fucked up.

"You know what, Brian? You ain't shit... Oh, and by the way, your daughter is doing good, and she's adjusting well to her new home and not being around your sorry ass anymore."

"Sam, fuck you, and she's not my daughter, and I wish you'd quit saying that shit. Did you have your wonderful King tested to see if he's her father? Because I ain't her daddy. Yeah, your secret is out, and I know all about y'all fucking when you came back after your brother's party. You should tuck your journal away better when you're writing about fucking another man. That's why after I read that shit, I started cheating on your hoe ass. It kills me how you're sitting here trying to act all high and mighty, like you're innocent, like you're the fucking victim when you stepped out on me first!" Brian yelled, taking a few steps toward me. I covered my mouth, surprised because I had no idea he knew about me and King but regardless of what he thinks, Kassidy's not King's daughter.

"Who does shit like this? How can you deny your own fucking flesh and blood? If you had any concerns about Kassidy's paternity, you should have said something when she was born so we could have done a DNA test.

But your sneaky ass walking around reading journals and shit, using me cheating as your way out. I wouldn't have cheated if your dick wasn't so small, bitch! Just write my daughter her check so I can sign the divorce papers!" I yelled after standing up in his face. I wanted to pick up a chair and beat his ass with it so bad.

"I'm not writing shit until I get a fucking DNA test because like I said, she's not my daughter. When she was born and I looked into that little girl's eyes, I knew she wasn't mine."

"Bitch, we can get the test done whenever you're ready, because I know she's not King's daughter, but now, since you want to be an ass, if we get a DNA test, then we're taking this shit to court, and I want what I'm owed, which is 50%. Now get the fuck out of my face!" I screamed and took a seat back on my chair. I looked at Damien, and he had a confused look on his face. I wanted to cry so fucking bad, but I refused to let Brian see me shed one tear because of his bitch ass.

"Hello, everyone. My name is Monica, and I'm the manager here at Starbucks. Sir, I'm going to have to ask you to leave the premises because you're disturbing the other customers. I've called the police, and they'll be here shortly." She informed Brian. He was pissed off she confronted him and said he had to go, but what really got him is that she didn't ask us to leave also. He looked around the store before his eyes landed on me, and he mugged me, and if looks could kill, I would have gone up in flames.

"This ain't over, Sam." Brian threatened as he took steps toward me. Damien quickly placed his hand on Brian's chest to halt his steps.

"Now you know that ain't about to happen. If you know like I know, you'll turn your ass around and walk the fuck up out or here.

Brian pushed Damien's hand and said, "Man, fuck you! You ain't running—"

Before he could finish, Damien punched his ass dead in the mouth. Brian stumbled back a few steps, and then he fell on the floor, dazed, and his mouth had blood running out of it like it was a river.

Damien kneeled in front of Brian while he was still on the floor, and low enough for just me and Brian to hear, Dame said, "Now, bitch, this is my last warning. I suggest you get your ass out of here before I pull my gun out and put you out of your misery." Brian struggled to stand, but when he was finally was able to stand up, he ran up out of here without saying another word.

"Sam, you good? "Damien questioned.

"Yeah," I replied.

"Come on. Let's head out before the police get here. You know I'm holdin', and I got some of that good shit on me," Damien said through a chuckle. I nodded my head, grabbed my purse and coffee, and I speed walked out of the door. I just hoped that would be the last time I had to see Brian, because if he caught me by myself, I didn't know what he would do to me.

BENNIE

Diane walked into my office and took a seat in one of the chairs positioned in front of my desk. Ever since Moe came to my office and told me about her being raped by my father, I'd been keeping my distance from Diane because I didn't know where my marriage stood. I hadn't answered any of her calls or texts, and I only responded to her emails that pertained to work. I knew she was upset with me about it, but that was just the way it had to be.

"Diane, what's up? I really don't have time to talk. I was on my way out of the door. I have a meeting I have to get to that I can't be late for," I asked her while stuffing my laptop and a few other things off my desk into my MCM bookbag.

Initially, she didn't say anything. She just stared at me like she was crazy as hell. A couple of minutes later, Diane stood up and walked over to my office door, closed it, and then locked it. She took a seat back in the chair in front of my desk, giving me unwavering eye contact.

"I need to talk to you about a few things with your wife being number one on my list of things we need to discuss." I knew the day Diane saw Moe in my office that she would have a million and one questions she would want to ask me because I hadn't told anyone at work that Moe had returned home. Especially since that was the last day I'd talked to Diane or met up with her. She'd been respectful enough not to try and hunt me down at work and put our business out there. That's the only reason I agreed to the affair. I knew Diane would be discreet and not involve others in what we had going on.

"Wait... my wife is none of your concern, and we've never really discussed Moe, and we're not about to start now, so Moe and my marriage are off the table for discussion. Now is there anything else you need to discuss with me?" I asked while walking around to the front of my desk. I leaned up against it and gave her my undivided attention.

"I just wanted to know when did she come back from Africa... and where does that leave us? Is she home for good, or is she going back abroad?" she hesitantly asked, looking down at her hands. Normally, Diane was very confident and outspoken, so seeing her so timid was new for me.

"Well, Diane, you know as well as I do there's no *us*, but Moe and I decided were going to work on our marriage. I'm sorry, and I know that's not what you want to hear, but it's the truth, and we've never lied to each other, and I'm not about to start now." In a way, I felt bad because normally I didn't discuss Moe with anyone but my family, but Diane caught me the day I told Moe I

12

wanted a divorce. I was in my feelings because I truly felt like my marriage was over, and I expressed that to Diane.

I tried my best not to cheat on Moe, but with the lack of intimacy, sex, and companionship over such a long period of time made it impossible for me to uphold my vows. I complained until I was blue in the face to my wife about needing her home with me, but it was like she had dismissed my feelings.

It had been a little over a year and a half since Moe had started volunteering when Diane and I started our affair. I felt like at that point, Moe was being selfish, and I didn't believe she cared about me or my feelings. I even had to grieve the loss of our children by myself for the longest, until Diane came into my life and helped me get through the tough times like the anniversary of their deaths, their birthdays, and holidays. Moe wasn't there for me, but Diane was, so I hoped my wife would understand and have some compassion for the situation when I told her about the affair.

I had worked with Diane for some time before I allowed anything to happen between the two of us. Our relationship went from colleagues to lovers the night of the hospital's annual Christmas party, which was always held at the hotel connected to the hospital. Diane had always been flirtatious with me ever since she'd met me, but I'd never fed into it. I don't know if it was because we weren't in a professional setting or what, but when she flirted with me that night, I was all for the bullshit. Toward the end of the night, I was busted and disgusted when Diane decided to pull me to the dance floor and twerk her fat ass on my dick, and that was it for me.

That night, I rented us a hotel room, and I took all the

frustrations I was currently dealing with out on her pussy all night long. When we woke up the next morning, she said she wanted to keep things strictly professional from that day forward. When we checked out of the hotel room, I had every intention of doing just that, but when I would go to work and see her, I couldn't. After sampling the goods, I was craving her ass like a drug, and I wanted more, but she wasn't down for it.

I chased her for about a month after the party before I broke her down, and she slept with me again. We'd been fucking ever since, and we were fucking like we were in relationship. We would get it in whenever and wherever we could—our offices, our cars, hotels, her house, and even my house. She'd spent nights with me at the house I shared with Moe, and we've had sex there, but only in the guest bedroom.

The reason I didn't tell Diane that Moe was home and why we had to stop messing around was because I didn't want to mess things up with her. In a way, I wanted to keep her on ice because I didn't know what was going to happen with my marriage.

That's why when Moe returned from Africa, I just slowed down how many times we would meet up after work and have sex, and I would only really communicate with her when we were at work. I just used KDB business as the reasoning for the change, and Diane never questioned it, but when Moe came up to the hospital and told me about my father raping her, I knew I had to stop everything I had going on with Diane.

"Look, Diane, I'm not going to beat around the bush. When I told Moe that I was filing for divorce, she immediately returned home so we could work on our marriage and hopefully save it. I'm not trying to purposely hurt you, but I have to end what we have going on and really put my all in trying to make my marriage work. I owe it to Moe to at least do that, and I can't do that if I'm still sleeping with and talking to you outside of work." As I looked into her eyes, I saw so much sadness like I had just crushed her whole world, but I had to tell her the truth.

"We've been fucking around for a little over a year... a fucking year Bennie, and then you tell me you're divorcing her, giving me hope that things between us could possibly move on to the next level. You started taking me out on dates, spending nights at my place, and I even introduced you to my son... my fucking son, Bennie! I allowed you in his life, and I allowed you to spend time with him, and he developed a bond with you. Then my stupid ass even allowed you to fuck me raw. What in the fuck was I thinking?" Diane stated with tears running from her eyes. I felt bad because Diane felt like I used her, and that wasn't the case at all.

The relationship with Diane was easy, and it just felt right when we were together. When it came to her son, I really enjoyed being around him because I missed my kids so much. He was a good kid, and she was a good mother to him.

"Fuck... Diane, you came into my life when I was lost and really needed someone to help me deal with the loss of my kids. I was wrong for even taking things there, because I was married, but Diane, I care about you, and I didn't expect for things to turn out like this. When I told Moe I was filing for divorce, I thought it would end with Moe signing the papers, and me and you could be together. I truly didn't think she would come home, because I thought that ship had sailed for the both of us." Diane didn't say anything. She just looked at me with saddened eyes as she placed her hand on her stomach.

Seeing Diane cry was tearing me up. As I pulled her hands away from her face and pulled her up out of the chair and into my chest, I began thinking about how hard it had been staying away from her and how hard it was going to be continuing to stay away from her. I tightened the hug I was giving her, and she really broke down in my arms, and it was making me realize why I shouldn't have started the affair in the first place.

"So why can't we just be together then?" Diane cried out.

"Because I owe it to my wife to try to see if we can work things out. I'm not asking you to wait on me or anything. I want you to do you, and if it's meant for us to be together, we will end up together."

Diane stood up and brushed her body across mine so she could grab some Kleenex off my desk, and when she did, I grabbed her into a hug, in which she barely returned the love. I put my face in the crook of her neck so I could smell her scent. For some reason, I always did that to her whenever I would see her because she always smelled so good to me.

Once I let her go, she wiped her eyes and blew her nose, and then she took a seat back in her chair. After sitting there quietly for about five minutes, I stood and walked around my desk so I could grab my stuff and head out. Before I made it around my desk, Diane started talking again. "Well, there's no easy way to tell you this but... um... Last week, I wasn't feeling that well. I didn't have an appetite at all, and I was barely able to keep food down. I went to the doctor—"

I cut her off before she could finish what she was saying. I nervously queried while shaking my head side to side, "Please don't tell me your pregnant, Diane! Please don't tell me your pregnant," I said not even really wanting a response.

Diane didn't say anything, but the tears started cascading down her cheeks, and that said it all for me. "Fuck!" I yelled, slamming my hand down on my desk, causing Diane to jump out of the chair she was sitting in. Diane took a few steps backward like she was scared that I was about to do something to her, and that pissed me off because she knew I would never hurt her.

"Yes. I found out I'm pregnant, and my doctor said I was ten weeks, and yes it's yours... I'm not keeping the baby, so you don't have to worry about your wife finding out," she nervously said. Diane grabbed her clipboard and phone off the chair as she headed toward the door.

"Diane, wait!" I didn't mean to say it so loud, because her scary ass jumped again. "Are you 100% sure that I'm the father, and if so, why are you trying to kill my seed?" I seriously questioned her because I thought we were better than that. The only reason I could think of that would make her want to terminate the pregnancy was because I wasn't the father.

"Do you really think I would lie to you about some-thing like this? You know me better than that, Bennie. You know you're the only person I've been fucking. I don't know if you're trying to insult me because I told you I was pregnant or what. I don't want to have your fucking baby because you're married and about to try to work things out with your fucking wife. I'm already a single mother, and it's hard, and adding another child to the mix will make it almost impossible for me, especially because we're not going to be together. I'll be doing it by myself most of the time, and I can't do it—no, I refuse to do it.

"I kept telling you I didn't want to have sex without protection, and you didn't listen to shit I was saying. Now look at the mess we're in," Diane said while throwing her hands in the air. She was right. We used condoms every time we had sex up until about six months before the pregnancy dilemma we were in. Diane let me slide up in that good shit without a condom on, and what the fuck she do that shit for? I'd been hooked ever since. We'd been using the pull-out method, but hell, the pussy was so good some days I couldn't even pull out, and honestly, I was surprised she hadn't gotten pregnant before then.

I walked back over to my desk and took a seat on the edge again, trying to figure out what I wanted to say or do. One thing I knew for sure was that I didn't want her to get an abortion. After being a father to two beautiful kids and then have them ripped away almost destroyed me. So the thought of her killing my seed was fucking with my head, and I didn't know if I could allow her to go through with that.

"Diane, come here, please," I said in a soft tone. Initially, she looked at me like I was crazy, and her body language was telling me she was scared. "Why all of a sudden you're acting like your scared of me?"

"Bennie, you're a dangerous man, and when people feel like they're being pushed into a corner, they're capable of doing some crazy shit to get out of it. I just don't want you to think I did this shit on purpose to drive a wedge between you and your wife, because I wouldn't do that. I ain't trappin' or beggin' a nigga to be with me."

"Diane, I know you didn't do this shit on purpose, because you get your own bag, and you too close to finishing school to risk fucking that up trying to trap me. Hell, if anything, it would be the other way around.

"You don't have to be scared of me because I would never hurt you. I care about you too much to cause you physical pain, love. Now can you please come here?" She hesitated, but then she started walking toward me, and when she got within an arm's reach, I pulled her toward me and into a hug.

I didn't know what I could say to make the situation right. "Look, I don't want you to kill my seed. You know what I've been through with my other two kids, and I can't even imagine you getting rid of something so precious. I wouldn't be able to live with myself knowing I allowed some shit like that to happen. I want this child, and I know it'll be hard, but I'll be there every step of the way. I promise you that."

I turned her around so her back was to my chest and placed both palms on her stomach, and she didn't say anything. She just placed her hands on top of mine. I placed my chin on her shoulder and said, "I don't know how to make this right, ma, but what I do know is this child will come first, above anyone or anything. I can promise you tha.t"

Diane stepped out of my grasp and took a seat on the arm of the chair in front of my desk, "Look, Bennie, I'm in love with you, and I can't have this baby, knowing you're not in love with me and that you're staying with your wife. I don't want to bring a child into this world in the middle of this mess. I also don't want my child being the reason your marriage ends either. I just think it's best if I have an abortion and we permanently end what we had going on. I might even apply for a position somewhere else in the hospital because it'll be too hard every day seeing you and being so close but so far away. I'm sorry, but I can't have this baby."

I took a seat in the other chair and waved for her to come over to me, but she didn't move. "Diane, come here, ma." I pulled her off the arm of the chair and pulled her over in front of me so my face was to her belly. I raised her shirt and kissed her stomach a couple of times and rubbed on it. "Please don't kill our child," I mumbled out.

"Bennie, please don't do this to me." She began trying to push my head away from her stomach, but I wasn't budging. "Don't you think this is hard for me too? This is my child *too* that's growing inside of me that I'm talking about killing," Diane groaned out as she tried to move from in front of me, but that shit wasn't happening because I put my hands on her ass keeping her there. "I'm sorry, but—"

"Listen, how about we meet up tonight, and we can discuss it more in depth. Just remember what I said. This baby comes before anybody and anything." I kissed her belly once more, and then I stood and placed a sensual kiss on her lips.

"I guess that's cool," she said with a little cute ass pout. Diane kissed me on my lips and walked out of my office.

I knew I was wrong as hell for what I was doing to Moe, but she put us there. I knew for a fact the baby Diane was carrying was mine, and I only questioned paternity because it was just an absentminded reaction to her announcing she was pregnant. I also knew Diane wouldn't keep the baby if I didn't choose to be with her and help her raise our child together, as a couple, but if I did that, I would hurt Moe. I had love for both women, but I was truly only in love with one, but I loved my seed more than I loved myself. So a big decision had to be made—my wife or my child.

13

MR. ROMELLO LEWIS

Romello

Ring! Ring! Ring! blared throughout the speakers in my car due to my Bluetooth being connected. Toy didn't answer, but instead, the call went to voicemail. I hoped this bitch wasn't trying to play me or fucked up and let Chris's bitch ass know we knew where he was hiding out. Once the call went to voicemail, I realized I had a text from Toy coming through.

Toy: Will call you right back!

I assumed she was sitting in front of Chris because she had sent me an instant reply.

Ring! Ring!

I didn't even allow it to ring the third time before I picked up the call.

"Toy, what the fuck going on? Why you couldn't answer the phone?" I asked, slightly pissed.

Toy blew a breath out before responding, "I'm sorry about that, but Chris has been on my ass since I talked to you last, so I've been trying to be really careful around his ass. He just went into the bedroom and took a call from his brother who just came into town... How much longer is it going to be before y'all come over and snatch his ass up? He's been acting extra crazy, and I don't know how much longer I can deal with this shit," she whispered through the phone.

"We're going to swoop through tonight after our meeting. I'll probably be sending you a text around ten or so, so keep your phone nearby and don't let him figure out what's going on. When we finish talking, erase my contact completely and all our text threads. I'll be calling you from a burner, so answer the fuckin' phone because my number won't be saved, alright?" I explained shit to her slow ass because I swear if she didn't answer the phone next time I called, I was going to kill her and Chris's ass.

"I already know what to do, but make sure y'all have my money when y'all come through to pick his ass up... Are we going to hook up after you finish with him tonight? You know I've been missing you, boo." I hung up on her ass without giving that bitch a second thought. I wasn't playing with Dame when I said I would never fuck her again. I truly meant that shit.

I decided to give Wayne a call and catch him up on what happened last night regarding Chris and Toy.

"Yo, what's up, Rome?" Wayne asked when he answered the phone.

"Not much. Aye, I want to talk to you about some shit that happened yesterday. Is this line clear?" We do that before we talk business over the phone with anyone because we never knew who was around or if the phones we were on was clear from bugs or anything else because you could never be too safe.

"No. Is it something important that can't wait?"

"Yeah," I answered.

"I'm going to call you right back on a clear line," Wayne said. He hung up on me, and a couple of minutes later he had called me back from an unknown number. If we felt a phone line wasn't clear, we would call Keys, and she somehow sends the call through a system that disguises the call with a different phone number, and then the program clears the line of any bugs, etc. Keys a bad bitch and an amazing asset to the team.

I answered the call. "Yeah?"

"What's up?" Wayne asked.

"Check it. Yesterday, Toy called me and says she heard about the bounty we have on Chris and that she wants to give us the information to catch him and claim the bounty."

"You fuckin' lying, my nigga," Wayne said, excited as hell.

"Nope. She told me he's been laying low at her spot and has been there since some shit he did to Tammy. I told her to keep him there, and if he leaves to call and let me know right away. I decided to go check the shit out for myself, so I rode by her spot. When I got there, I snuck around the side of the house and looked through the window, and the bitch Toy was getting her back blown out by Chris, the same nigga that was fuckin' her friend. I swear hoes ain't loyal, and that's why I quit fuckin' with her ass a while ago," I mumbled that last part, but I knew his overhearing ass heard me.

"Is he still there?" Wayne questioned.

"Yeah. I just talked to her, and she said he's gotten suspicious and been watching her movements like a hawk. I sent a few niggas over there to sit on her spot, and I told her we would be there tonight to swoop his ass." I couldn't wait until Chris was handled.

"Alright, that's cool. I'll get a few niggas together, and we can handle that shit after the meeting. Call me if anything changes before we meet up later. Is Damien with you?"

"No. I was supposed to pick him up, but he said he had something to take care of first. We were supposed to meet up at the Hubb and leave out from there to handle that business in Akron. So I'm headed to the Hubb now. You sure you don't want to move on Chris now?" I curiously asked because it had been so hard to track the nigga down up until then.

"Nah, because if he's been there all this time, he has nowhere to go, so he ain't going nowhere. Alright, call me if you need anything or if shit changes." With that, Wayne hung up, and I headed over to the Hubb so I could get my day started. Damien and I had a few weapon deliveries we needed to handle, with one of those deliveries being in Akron, and Akron wasn't just around the corner. It was a nice little ride. Lieutenants normally handled deliveries because they involved money being transferred, but since it would be the first delivery with that new customer, Dame needed to tag along.

～

Damien and I had just arrived for the scheduled meeting at the Hubb. It seemed like it took us forever to deliver the weapons to a crew in Akron and make it back to Cleveland in time for this meeting, and I was tired as fuck. I was pissed when we hit rush hour because traffic was deadlocked, and we wouldn't had even been in the middle of that shit if Damien didn't have to "handle" some shit earlier. It took him another two hours to make it to the Hubb this morning, causing us to be about three hours behind schedule. Then to top it off, I was horny as hell, and I couldn't get no pussy until after we handled Chris's ass when the meeting was over with. And the Chris shit was liable to take all night, and I was the type of nigga that needed to pussy or head at least once in the morning and once at night. That's the reason my attitude was so fucked up all day. Pussy was like a drug to me, and I constantly needed my fix.

I decided to at least try and setup some plans for that night before the meeting started, just in case shit ran smoothly and it didn't take all night to get shit done. I sent out a text to a good friend of mine named Harmoney to see what she had planned for the night. I had been fucking around with her for about a year, and she was cool as hell. The only problem was it was hard to catch up with her because she was always working or some shit.

If I ever decided to settle down, it would be with her because she ain't have no kids, she went out and got her own bag, and she grinded harder than some niggas I knew. She was a nurse, and she had just started her own home-care business, plus she worked PRN at University Hospital and Cleveland Clinic's emergency room.

Me: How's your day going, beautiful? Wanted to meet up with you tonight. Do you have any plans?

I waited for a response, and I started thinking about our last encounter when I almost put a fucking ring on her shit. It had to be illegal somewhere for a woman to be a boss, no kids, gorgeous as hell, and pussy tight and muthafuckin' right, and let's not discuss her fuckin' neck game. The only problem I had with her was she was ready to settle down, and I wasn't. Plus, she refused to make me a priority until I decided to settle down and be monogamous. She had other niggas she fucked, and she only dealt with me on her terms, not mine. If the pussy wasn't so good, I would've probably said fuck her, but how she had my toes curling when she sucked my dick the last time I saw her... I decided to wait in line with the rest of the niggas.

My phone alerted me that I just received a text, which pulled me out of my devious, sexual thoughts of her fine ass.

Harmoney: Hey. Haven't seen you in a while. I'm not free tonight, but I'll cancel those plans to kick it with you. What time would you like to meet up?

Me: I have some important shit to take care of, but I should be done between 10:00-10:30.

Harmoney: That's cool because I don't get off until 7:30, so it'll give me time to freshen up. Are you sure about this, because I don't want to cancel my plans and you never show like you've done so many times before? If you do, I'm done, and I'm not going to deal with you anymore.

Me: Don't fuckin' threaten me. You know I don't like that shit, but I'll take it out on your jaws and pussy tonight! You know what type of work I do and what I'm building, so don't

be like that, ma. I try my best, but as of now, I'll be there. Keep
that pussy tight for a real nigga.

Harmoney: *Please punish me! I've been a bad girl!*

When I talked to Dame the night before, it made me
look at shit going on in my life, and I felt like it was time
for me to settle down and have some kids. I wasn't ready
for all that marriage shit, but I was ready to try the one-
woman thing again.

I turned my attention to King, Damien, and Beast.
They were about to start the meeting.

King stood and said, "Okay, we're about to get started,
everyone. I'm giving y'all a fair warning, because we don't
want a repeat of previous meetings. Do. Not. Speak.
Unless. You're. Given. The. Floor. That shit is mad disrespectful, and disrespect can cause only one thing to
happen to you this evening—a bullet between your eyes,
bottom line!" King yelled, slamming his hand down on
the table.

"Well, we called this meeting just for our lieutenants
because we're about to change some things up from this
point forth. Things have been running better since our
last meeting, but we need them to run damn near perfect
in order to meet our monthly goals." King stopped and
looked around the room, making eye contact with every
lieutenant sitting at the conference table.

"First things first, it's time to clean house. I blame
myself for the bullshit we're going through with members
that's disloyal. I allowed people into KDB that didn't
deserve to be let in and represent those three letters.

"I want every lieutenant to sit down with Wayne and
discuss every crew member under your command. I

allowed a few people to slip through that shouldn't be representing KDB. So if you have anybody who's not holding their own, I need those individuals' memberships terminated ASAP. Beast, you have the floor," King said right before he sat down, and Beast stood up and began.

"First, I want to commend everyone for improving how things flow in your house and with your crews, and I also see how those improvements have increased profit in all six houses. Starting next week, lieutenants will be partnered up with another lieutenant from another house, and those two will rotate houses every week. The second in command will not rotate but will answer to both men and will maintain the flow of that trap under your supervision. This will build stronger crews, and you'll always have someone of higher authority able to take over at the drop of a dime. We have our standard rules and regulations across the board, but the two lieutenants will develop their own set of rules for those two traps," Beast said before taking a seat in his chair.

Damien stood and addressed the room. "So I'm going to be short. I have only two lieutenants and seven other crew members under y'all that work with weapons. That has to change because with the increase of our weapons inventory means the increase in sales, and I need men who know what they're doing to help me with that. I want you to ask your crew members if anybody would like to convert over. It's easier to take someone already a member and transfer them over to my area than to train someone who has no knowledge about anything KDB. Let Romello know by the beginning of next week so they can get thoroughly trained, because our new shipments start next month. That's it!" He sat down, and Wayne stood and continued on with the meeting.

Wayne went on for about another fifteen minutes or so, but I really wasn't paying attention. I was mapping out in my head how things were going to play out when we went to pick Chris's punk ass up.

"Does anybody have any questions?" Wayne asked as he looked around the room, waiting to see if anyone responded. I guess nobody had any questions, because didn't nobody say anything. Wayne continued on, "Would any of the heads like to add anything before I dismiss everyone?" Beast and Damien responded with a no. "

King, do you have anything to add?" Beast asked loudly so he could get his attention.

"Nah, I'm good," King answered.

"OK! Everyone's dismissed but Romello. Can you stay after so we can discuss a few more things with the heads? Everybody else, you're dismissed." With that, everyone stood and walked out of the conference room.

It was time to deliver the news to King that he had been waiting to hear for a good minute. Hopefully, things would go as planned, and we could swoop in, snatch Chris ass up, and be on our way. Then I could dip out and go kick it with my girl, Money. Money was the nickname I liked to call her ever since we first started messing around. At the time, I felt it was a perfect fit because her ass stayed chasing a bag, just like me.

Our norm for the entire year I fucked with her was all about fucking. We would fuck, and afterward, I took my black ass home, but I wanted to do things a little differ-ent. I wanted to get to know Money, and I hoped like hell she wanted to get to know me also because I was ready to take things to the next level.

14

KING

"King, do you have anything you need to add?" Beast asked, pulling me out of my thoughts.

"Nah, I'm good," I answered. I really hadn't been paying much attention to what was going on during the meeting because I was so focused on meeting up with Sam, and hopefully clearing the air between the two of us.

"Okay, everyone's dismissed," Wayne announced, and then he turned to Romello and requested, "Aye, Romello and Main, I need y'all to stay behind so we can talk to the heads real quick." Romello nodded at Wayne, but Main looked between Wayne and Romello like he was confused and didn't know what was going on.

I was glad Wayne asked Rome and Main to stay afterward because I needed to talk to everybody about what happened the night Bennie's father was killed, because Bennie was the only person who knew about the latest shit Chris had done.

I felt like I owed the people that were left in the

conference room an explanation, but Bennie and I decided we wanted to wait until we had more information and knew the whole story behind the drug and how it affected my me.

"Aye, I wanted to talk to y'all about some information that was brought to my attention, and it's about Chris, the biggest thorn in my fuckin' side." I looked around the table, and everyone was giving me their undivided attention, so I continued, "Well, it turns out that Chris switched my vitamins for a drug that attacked my brains nervous system, and that's why I'd been acting crazy as hell."

"How was he able to get that shit off? I know you ain't invite the nigga over for tea and crumpets or some shit like that," Dame's stupid ass questioned.

"He used Tammy's keycard to gain access to his condo," Bennie offered up, looking disgusted as hell. Bennie was pissed because he knew the medical ramifications from me consuming too much of the drug. The liver damage was irreversible, and there was no telling what other shit could come up in the future.

"That bitch should've been took a dirt nap a long fuckin' time ago, and King, I've respected your decision to allow that hoe to breathe up 'til this point, but that shit ends today. We can't keep overlooking the shit she does because she's KJ's mother. That hoe got to go," Dame said with finality, and I couldn't do shit but respect it, because he was right.

"Bro, I agree with Dame on this one," Bennie voiced as he leaned back in his chair.

"The drug Chris used is a drug that, long story short, heightens the feeling of emotions we feel when our bodies go through the fight-or-flight response. So whenever King would have an increased amount of adrenaline in his bloodstream, it would make his brain overly sensitive to any emotion, like anger, which caused him to act out of character." Bennie stopped talking, and then he looked up at me for approval to continue.

"You can finish," I told Bennie.

"Well, a bad side effect of the medication if too much is consumed is organ damage, and King's test results showed he's in the beginning stages of liver failure," Bennie angrily spat.

"Is the damage permanent, or is it something you can do to reverse the effects, Bennie?" Wayne queried.

"The damage that's been done is permanent, and there's nothing I can do about that, but I started King on some medication that could possibly keep the damage from getting any worse. I'll keep my eye on him though." Bennie informed everybody.

"What are we going to do about Tammy's trifling ass?" Damien questioned while looking me dead in the eyes, almost as if he was trying to intimidate me. I should've fucked with him some, but I didn't have time, so I put him out of his misery.

Everybody looked at me with questionable eyes. "I handled that situation already, and she finally has that beautiful Lake E view she's always wanted."

"Nigga, you good though?" Damien's bipolar ass asked me, looking concerned.

"Nigga, you need to make your bipolar ass mind the fuck up. Aw, you concerned about Big Daddy, huh?" I said through chuckles. "I'm good though. That ship sailed a long time ago, and the only reason she was still breathing was because of my son."

I turned toward Wayne and Romello, giving them my undivided attention. "Romello came across Chris's location yesterday." Wayne informed us.

"Did y'all snatch his bitch ass up already?" I challenged.

"I wasn't able to grab him last night because it was too many eyes around, and I didn't want to bring no heat our way, so instead, I put two teams on the house. Flow and Reese are stationed in a car parked two houses down, and Mike and Solo are stationed in a car behind Toy's house."

"Where has he been hiding, and how did you find out his location?"

Wayne chuckled before Romello answered, "Toy called—"

"Toy? Tammy's friend Toy?" I questioned after I unintentionally cut him off, because he couldn't have been talking about Tammy's friend Toy. She didn't even know Chris. That started the wheels in my head a turning. I wondered if Tammy's lying ass had anything to do with him being at Toy's spot.

Mello went on to tell us how he found out where Chris was.

"But check it! What's crazy is, when I stopped by Toy's last night to make sure she wasn't lying about Chris being there, I looked through the window, and I saw them fuckin' on the couch." Rome informed us. I wasn't surprised because Toy tried to fuck me on multiple occasions, and she ended up sucking my dick one night when I was drunk as hell. The next day, she tried to blackmail me saying she tell Tammy if I didn't give her some money.

Before she could finish with the threat, I had shoved my gun down her throat and turned the tables on her ass real quick.

"Did you want to roll with us to pick his bitch ass up?" Wayne asked me.

I answered, "Nah, I'm good. You, Romello, and Main take a couple of people over to Toy's with you and pick Chris's ass up and bring him back here. Make sure it's clean because we can't afford any mistakes right now, and no witnesses, including Toy. Set fire to the house, and have Keys wipe any cameras within a mile radius of the house," I ordered.

Wayne and Romello walked out of the workroom, headed toward Toy's place.

"Aye, I need to talk to y'all about some shit that went down this morning while I was with Sam," Damien said, piquing my attention when he said Sam's name.

"Sam and I met up at Starbucks because I wanted to talk to her about Camille. I'm assuming her husband followed her from the house, because while Sam and I were sitting down choppin' it up, he walked his white ass up in there like he owned the place. He approaches our table and confronts her about their divorce and Kassidy's paternity. He said some shit that blew my whole fuckin' mind," Damien said while laughing to himself and shaking his head from side to side.

Curiously, I asked, "What did he say?"

"He said that he knew that Sam fucked you the night of Bennie's birthday party—"

"Wait, what?" I asked after cutting Dame off. "How in the hell did he find out about that? I know Sam didn't just offer up that information to him. We didn't tell nobody about that night," I queried.

"Anybody with eyes knew y'all had plans on fucking that night, and knowing your nasty ass, you probably fucked her in the bathroom during the party." Dame smirked.

"Can we please not discuss my sister fucking King in a nasty ass bathroom at the club?" Bennie mugged the hell out of me, but I couldn't do shit but laugh.

"But to answer your question, he said he read it in Sam's journal, and he also said, he's 99.9% sure that you *are* the father!" Damien said, laughing, but I didn't find anything funny about what he said.

"Did he say that shit because he's pissed, or is it something that he truly believes? Did he have a DNA test done or something?" Bennie asked, taking the words right out of my mouth.

"He really believes that shit, but from the stuff Sam told me, it seems like Brian's just trying to get out of being her father so he'll be free and clear to marry his fiancée who's currently pregnant with his kid. His wack ass plans on signing over his rights to Kassidy over to Sam when he signs the divorce papers." Damien disclosed.

"That's some weak shit, and Sam and Kassidy deserve better," Bennie spat. "Who the fuck gives up their rights to their seed for a bitch? I'm beating the brakes off that nigga when I see him, and he better hope I walk away not ending his pathetic ass life!" Bennie slammed his hand down on the table mad as hell. "Dame, please tell me you beat his ass?" Bennie angrily asked. I would've been just as mad if a nigga did that shit to my sister, if I had one.

Damien's crazy ass started laughing, causing Bennie

and I to laugh too. We already knew he did something to Brian. His ass had no chill, so I knew he laid hands on that nigga, and he didn't give a fuck who witnessed that shit either. I didn't either, because we're protected across the board, but we tried to stay off twelve's radar.

"I blessed him with a nice two-piece combo, and believe me, I wanted to do more, but the manager had already called twelve, and a nigga was ridin' dirty as hell, so I couldn't tag that ass like I really wanted to," Damien said through laughs. "But believe me, his jaw will still be feeling me in the morning."

"Aye, Bennie, when is Kassidy's birthday?" I questioned Bennie because I couldn't remember to save my life.

Bennie responded, "Here we go with this bullshit again... Kassidy's birthday is May 5th."

"If I had sex with Sam the night of your birthday party, is there a possibility that Kassidy could be mine?" I questioned because as I counted backward, I came to the conclusion that it was a possibility that I could really be Kassidy's father.

"Yeah, it's a chance, but to really answer that question you'll have to talk to Sam to find out her due date, but you know as well as I do that if Sam thought it was a possibility you were Kassidy's father, she would have told you. Sam would never keep nothing like that away from you, even if it meant her marriage ending."

Everything Bennie said were straight facts, but I needed to hear it from the horse's mouth. I pulled out my phone to call Sam because I needed to talk to her immediately about Kassidy's paternity.

"Hello?" Sam answered the phone, sounding sexy as hell.

"Hey, ma. This King. Can I slide through real quick? I need to talk to you about something, and it's very important," I asked while walking toward the door.

"Would this have something to do with what happened when I was with Damien at Starbucks, and what was said about Kassidy being your daughter?" she asked, already knowing the answer to that question.

"Yeah."

"You can come over, because it's something I've been wanting to discuss with you, and I think we should put everything on the table once and for all. I'm headed home now, but Kassidy and Nina are there, and I'll tell her to let you in because you're going to make it there before me." Sam informed me, and I drove all the way to her house in silence, thinking about the possibilities. Once I made it to Sam's, I sent Damien and Bennie a text message letting them know I left and where I was going, but I was pretty sure they already knew what was going on when I walked out of the conference room without saying a word.

Me: *Made a quick run to Sam's. Text me when my gift arrives!*

Bennie: *Figured. Will do.*

Damien: *You're so whipped! Will do.*

Damien got on my fuckin' nerves because his ass never missed a fuckin' beat.

Preston Paris: *We need to talk before the night ends. I have the information you requested.*

Even though I had Keys looking into Chris's past and his whereabouts, I still didn't want to put all my eggs in

one basket. That's why I asked Preston if he would look
into finding Chris, and I asked if he could get me Chris's
closed juvenile records. I thought it might have been
something his records that would put us closer to
answering the question: why was he doing all of this?

WHEN I PULLED up to Sam's house, I parked on the curb
directly in front of her house, but I didn't see her car
parked on the street, so I just assumed she hadn't made it
yet. I got out and walked up the walkway and climbed the
few steps that led to her front porch, and as I rang the
doorbell, I admired the nice little condo she purchased in
Little Italy.

I heard the locks turning, and when the door
opened it was an older woman whom I'd never seen
before. "Hello. My name is Nina. I'm Kassidy's nanny,"
the beautiful, older woman said with her hand extended
out for me to shake, I accepted the gesture and shook
her hand.

"I'm Kingston. Has Sam made it home yet? She
should be expecting me. I talked to her not too long ago."
Nina opened the door wider and gestured for me to come
inside, and once I crossed the threshold, she closed the
door and locked it behind me.

"I know. She called and said you might beat her here
before she makes it home because she was caught in traffic. She told me to let you in and make sure you're
comfortable. Her crazy butt sent a picture of you and
everything," she said through laughter. "She doesn't play
when it comes to Kassidy's safety."

"I understand. Nowadays you can never be too safe," I responded.

"You can have a seat in the living room. The television is already on and the remote is on the couch." I followed her into the living room and took a seat. "Would you like something to drink—beer, wine, water? I think we have apple juice, which is Kassidy's favorite, so Sam keeps it on hand."

"No. I'm good, but thanks for offering."

I took a seat on the couch, and Nina walked out of the room, and it sounded like she went upstairs. After almost ten minutes, she came back into the living room and asked, "King, can you help me take some of these heavy boxes upstairs to Sam's room please?" she asked so nicely that there was no way I could say no.

"Yeah, which boxes you need me to take upstairs?" I asked her as I followed her out of the living room.

"Can you grab these two boxes right here and take them up to Samantha's room for me. They're a little too heavy for me." I nodded my head and grabbed the boxes and followed Nina, who was carrying a smaller box upstairs herself.

When we walked into Sam's room, I looked around, and I was really impressed because the colors she used to decorate her bedroom were my favorite three colors— gray, black, and white.

"You can place the boxes over there along her wall, and I'm going to take this box to Kassidy's room really quick," Nina said as she turned and headed out of the bedroom.

"Nina, I'm ready for you to read me my story now!" I heard a little girl yell as Nina exited Sam's room, and I walked over to the wall that Nina pointed out, and I placed the boxes on the floor. When I went to stand, I noticed the top box said *journals.* My mind immediately flashed back to when Damien said that Sam's husband knew we fucked because he read her journal. Now the gangsta in me was telling me to stand the fuck up and walk out of her bedroom, but I couldn't because I needed answers, and I knew the answers I was looking for probably lie in that box. *Fuck it,* I thought.

I opened the top of the box, and it was a lot of stuff packed to the rim, but the composition notebooks immediately caught my eye. It was six of them, and the one on top was titled *grad school,* so I shuffled through them until I came across the one that was titled *12th grade,* and immediately, I knew that was the grade all the shit went down with us. I grabbed the journal out of the box and flipped through the pages quickly. I felt like shit for reading her private thoughts, but I needed to know what really happened. I flipped through the pages and stopped when I came across the date, August 12th. That was the day Sam missed school, and she called me and broke up with me out of the blue, without any explanation of why.

August 12th: *This is the first day I had the energy to write in my journal since I found out I was pregnant. The last week has been unbearable, and I don't know how much longer I can go through with living like this.*

The day my father found out I was pregnant with King's baby, he beat my mother's ass really bad, and he beat me within inches of my own life. I'd never seen Max lose control in the manner he did almost two weeks ago. The entire time he beat me, all I could do was try to cover my stomach and try to protect my baby as much as I could, just in case the devil had a slither of human decency and allowed me to keep my baby.

He's such a sick fuck. I truly believe he was trying to make me have a miscarriage so he wouldn't have to pay for an abortion. I had my initial appointment at Planned Parenthood exactly five days ago. I didn't know the abortion process was a two-day process. The first appointment, I had to take a pregnancy test. They did an ultrasound to see how far along I was, and then I had to sit through hearing my baby's heartbeat.

That shit killed me because it made the baby real and made me realize I had a life growing inside of me, a baby that King and I made from love, and when I got home that evening, I begged my father to let me keep my baby, but he said no.

I had to stop reading because it was like I could hear Sam speaking the words as I silently read them. I was about to close the journal, but something stopped me. I felt I owed it to Sam to finish reading and get her entire truth.

August 12ᵗʰ continued: *Today's been the worst day of my life because my father forced me to go through with the abortion, and he threatened to take my life, King's life, and my mother's life if I told anyone about the abortion.*

I cried during the entire procedure, and afterward, Max made me call King and break up with him. My heart is so broken right now, and I don't know how I'm going to be able to go on as if nothing happened.

My heart and womb are so empty, and I have nothing at all. Regardless of the bullshit my father keeps saying, I know for a fact that King and I would've been good parents to our child, but I must believe God does everything for a reason. Maybe God didn't want my child to have to endure the hell

I've been living in. I just wish I had at least one person to help me through all of this.

After I broke up with King, my father said I could no longer be friends with Camille, and I feel like I have no one out here in this cold, cold world.

As I read the journal entry, I got a little choked up because I could feel the pain she was experiencing through every word she wrote like I was right in front of her while she was telling me her story. I was having images of her sitting in her room writing it, and I was devastated. What took me out was the ultrasound picture that was taped underneath it.

As I outlined my child's body with my finger, my heart broke for the life that we loss, *my seed*. How could someone force their daughter to kill their baby? "Who the fuck does shit like that?" I whispered to myself.

I closed her journal and put it back in the box labeled *journals* and exited Sam's room, feeling like the dumbest nigga on the fuckin' planet. As I walked down the hall, I heard a little girl, who I assumed was Kassidy and Nina talking about Kass's father. I stopped walking and listened because I wanted to hear what they were going to say about his weak ass. I leaned against the wall when I heard Kassidy start asking Nina questions.

"G-Ma Nina, me friend Julie said her daddy reads to her, and he tells her stories, and he plays with her, but me daddy Brian don't. Why, G-Ma? Was I a bad girl? G-Ma, I promise I'll be a good girl from now on," Kassidy promised. Man, oh man this some sad shit. This little girl was blaming herself for why her daddy a fuck boy and not stepping up like he was supposed to.

"No, Kassidy. Don't you ever blame yourself for how your father act—"

Kassidy cut her off and said, "He said he's not me daddy, and he told me daddy name, and that me Mommy lies to him." Man, I swore on KJ, I was putting a bullet between that nigga Brian's eyes if I ever crossed paths with him. That shit was brutal to listen to, and I didn't know how much longer I could stand there and listen to that bullshit.

I hadn't realized I moved in Kassidy and Nina's line of sight until Kassidy asked, "G-Ma, who's that?" Kassidy pointed her finger in my direction. Nina turned around on the bed so she could see me, and when Nina and I made eye contact, she smiled at me. I took a few steps forward and walked completely into the room, and I was mesmerized, because Kassidy was the most beautiful little girl I'd ever seen in my life.

Kassidy was sitting Indian style on her bed with her Doc McStuffins pajamas on. She had the most beautiful straight, jet-black hair that was hanging to the middle of her back. Her skin complexion was way lighter than Sam's caramel complexion. When Kassidy made eye contact with me, her eyes were amazing, and I'd never seen anything like it before. Her eye color was green like Sam's, but she had hazel specks in them, but what made them truly unique was the gray color that outlined the green part of her eyes. Kassidy smiled, causing me to smile because I saw quarter-sized dimples in her cheeks. Kassidy was the replica of the little girl I used to imagine Sam and I would have.

Kassidy climbed off the side of her bed and anchored her body on it.

"Are you Kassidy?" I asked, taking a few steps into the room, and Kass nodded her head yes while taking a few steps in my direction, stopping right in front of me.

"Mister, are you here to see me mommy? She's not home yet... What's your name?" Kass asked, looking up at me.

I bent down and dropped a knee to the floor so I was eye level with her. I answered, "My name is Kingston, but everyone calls me King... Has anyone ever told you you're such a beautiful little girl?" Her eyes got big as hell, and I could see the excitement dancing in them. *Damn, she's a beautiful little girl. How can her father not love and adore her? If she was my daughter, she would have me wrapped around her little finger,* I thought.

Kassidy started jumping in place, and then she jumped up and wrapped her arms around my neck. She screamed, "You're me daddy! Brian said me daddy's name is King, so you got to be me daddy, right?"

I felt like I was in *The Twilight Zone,* and I didn't have a clue of what was going on at that point. How was I supposed to tell this little girl her shit-face father was a liar, and I wasn't her fuckin' father and break her little heart?

"Daddy, can you please pick me up!" she excitedly yelled. *Fuck!* I didn't know what the right thing was to do, so I looked over at Nina, and she had tears rolling down her face, and I knew it was because she felt sorry for Kass.

Under my breath, I mumbled, "Fuck it." I picked her up in my arms, and she hugged me tightly around my neck, and I returned the gesture. It brought tears to my eyes because it made me think about KJ and how he would hug me and hang off my neck sometimes. *Man, oh man do I miss my little man.* I heard a sound from behind me, and when I turned around, I saw Sam standing in the door wiping away tears.

"What's going on in here, munchkin?" Sam said after she kissed Kassidy and grabbed her out of my arms. Kassidy didn't want to go, but I didn't want to overstep and say the wrong thing.

"Mommy, this me daddy. This me daddy." Sam looked at Kassidy confused as hell, and then she turned and looked at me like I was the one who told Kass that shit.

"Munch, what are you talking about? Your father is Brian," Sam said with confusion laced in her voice and on her face.

"No!" Kassidy yelled. "This me daddy, King!" Kassidy said such finality. "Brian said that me daddy name King, and he said he not me daddy, Mommy." I could see the sadness wash all over Sam's face because of what Kass said. Kass reached for me to grab her out of Sam's arms, and I did because Sam was barely holding it together.

"Munch... I'm not sure why Daddy Brian told you that, but he is your—"

I cut Sam off and asked her if we could step out so I could talk to her. She looked at Kassidy, me, then Nina before she agreed to step out and talk with me. I placed Kassidy on her feet, and she ran over to her bed so she could sit next to Nina.

"Kassidy, me and your mom is going to go downstairs and talk for a minute, okay?" Sam and I walked out of the room, and once in the hallway, she closed the bedroom door. I followed her downstairs into the living room, and I took a seat on the couch, but I didn't even let her ass hit the couch all the way before I asked her the million-dollar question.

"Sam, is Kassidy my fuckin' daughter?" Initially, Sam didn't say anything. She started playing with her hands nervously, and when she stopped and got ready to speak, my cell phone started ringing. *That's some bad timing for that ass,* I thought, and when I looked down at the screen, the caller ID said it was Mello, so I already knew what time it was.

"Look, I gotta answer this," I said right before I answered my phone. I turned my back to Sam and took a few steps toward the kitchen.

"Hello?" I spoke into the phone.

"Hey. I picked up that gift you asked me for," Mello responded.

"Alright. I'll head your way." I hung up, and when I looked at Sam, she was sitting there with tears still running down her face and nervously playing with her hands. From previous experiences, I knew she only did that when she was scared about something.

"Sammie, I know we can't have the conversation we need to have, but I want to apologize for putting my hands on you, and I promise I'll never do no shit like that again. I don't have time to do a lot of explaining, but when I choked you, somebody had drugged me. I would never purposely hurt you like that. I sat down next to her, and it was like she was trying to avoid eye contact with me. I started to get worried, and I began thinking that what Brian told Kassidy may have been the truth.

I pulled her body into mine and placed my chin on the top of her head and asked her, "Will you accept my apology, and do you forgive me, ma?" Sam didn't say anything. She just leaned her head into my chest and wrapped her arms around me.

"King I'm so sorry—"

I cut her off before she could go any further. "I just wanted to apologize for laying my hands on you. We can discuss everything else when I come back, if that's cool with you? Can you do me a favor and wait to talk to Kassidy about what your wack ass baby daddy told her? I need to go handle some shit at the Hubb, but I'll make it quick so we can finish this conversation." I grabbed her under her chin and tilted her head back so I could look into her eyes.

"Yes. Just call me when you're on your way, okay?"

"I will." I gave her two small pecks on her lips and then headed for the door.

"Listen out for your phone because I'll call when I'm headed back this way." Once outside, I climbed into my midnight-blue G-Wagon and peeled off, headed toward the Hubb. The entire ride there, I thought about how I wanted Sam and I to handle Kassidy's paternity. I didn't think I had it in me to break that little girl's heart and tell her I'm not her father!

15

DAMIEN

"Aye, I need to talk to y'all about some shit that went down this morning while I was with Sam." I looked directly at King to see if I got his attention, and like I thought, his whipped as turned, giving me his undivided attention. "Sam and I met up at Starbucks because I wanted to talk to her about Camille. I'm assuming her husband followed her from the house, because while Sam and I were sitting down choppin' it up, he walked his white ass up in there like he owned the place. He approaches our table and confronts her about their divorce and Kassidy's paternity. He said some shit that blew my whole fuckin' mind," I said, laughing to myself and shaking my head from side to side.

"What did he say?" King questioned.

"He said that he knew that Sam fucked you the night of Bennie's birthday party—"

"Wait, what?" King asked, looking confused, after he so rudely cut me off. "How in the hell did he find out about that? I know Sam didn't offer up that information to him. We didn't tell nobody about that night." King sat there, looking crazy as hell, but he really was crazy if he thought we didn't know he and Sam fucked that night.

"Anybody with eyes could tell y'all had plans on fucking that night, and knowing your nasty ass, you probably fucked her in the bathroom during the party." I smirked, letting the cat out of the bag.

"Can we please not discuss, my sister fucking King in a nasty ass bathroom at the club?" Bennie looked like he wanted to throw up in his mouth.

"But to answer your question, he said he read it in Sam's journal, and he also said he's 99.9% sure that you *are* the father!" I tried my best to impersonate Maury's ass.

"Did he say that shit because he's pissed, or is it something that he truly believes? Did he have a DNA test done or something?" Bennie questioned.

"He really believes that shit, but from the stuff Sam told me, it seems like Brian's just trying to get out of being her father so he'll be free and clear to marry his fiancée, who's currently pregnant with his kid. His wack ass plans on signing over his rights to Kassidy over to Sam when he signs the divorce papers." I disclosed.

"That's some weak shit, and Sam and Kassidy deserve better," Bennie spat. "Who the fuck gives up their rights to their seed for a bitch? I'm beating the brakes off that nigga when I see him, and he better hope I walk away not ending his pathetic ass life!" Bennie slammed his hand down on the table mad as hell. "Dame, please tell me you beat his ass?" Bennie angrily asked.

"I blessed him with a nice two-piece combo, and believe me, I wanted to do more, but the manager had already called twelve, and a nigga was ridin' dirty as hell, so I couldn't tag that ass like I really wanted to," I said through laughs. "But believe me, his jaw will still be feeling me in the morning."

"Aye, Bennie, when is Kassidy's birthday?" King questioned Bennie, because I already knew that nigga's mind was racing, but I believe Sam when she said her husband was Kassidy father.

Bennie responded, "Here we go with this bullshit again... Kassidy's birthday is, May 5th."

"If I had sex with Sam the night of your birthday party, is there a possibility that Kassidy could be mine?" King questioned Bennie as the rest of us looked at Bennie, awaiting his answer.

"Yeah, it's a chance, but to really answer that question, you'll have to talk to Sam to find out her due date, but you know as well as I do that if Sam thought it was a possibility you were Kassidy's father, she would have told you. Sam would never keep nothing like that away from you, even if it meant her marriage ending." Everything Bennie said were straight facts.

KING PICKED up his cell phone and called Sam then he put the call on speaker. "Hello?" Sam answered the phone.

"Hey, ma. This King. Can I slide through really quick? I need to talk to you about something, and it's very important," King asked Sam as he walked out the conference room.

King left just Bennie and me waiting for Wayne and Romello to return. I grabbed my burner because I needed to check on a couple of spots since Romello, Wayne, and Main went to snatch up Chris.

It was crazy how we spent a lot of money to get our traps connected to the tunnel system, but when it was said and done, we could only connect three of the traps to the underground system. We should have been up and running by now, but Chris made sure that shit was impossible by planting a whole bunch of viruses and bugs within our central computer system.

Keys and Mac had to basically reset the entire system, but it seemed like every day they would find something else that he planted. It was crazy because Chris took his time and planned this shit out over a year, planting seeds here and there, and that's why I felt the attack was personally setup to hurt King. Hell, Chris even fucked his wife, so you know the shit is personal as hell, but it still leaves the question: why is Chris doing all of this?

Since Wayne, Mello, and Main went out to scoop Chris up, I decided to check in in with a few of our workers, and make sure everything moving smoothly.

Me: How's business?

LaVelle: Good!

Me: How's business?

Kurt: Slow.

Me: How's business?

Jason: Above, re...

Me: 60.

The trap on 129th and Arlington had been jumpin' ever since Main took over the house, and they were moving a lot of product. Jason said he needed a re-up, so I assumed they must be close to being out of work. Main was bringing in damn near double of what Chris was bringing in when he ran the house.

I let Jason know somebody would be there in an hour to drop some work off. Before I could make my next call, a call came in from Chanel, and the only reason I answered it was because I hadn't seen DJ in a couple of days.

"What's up, Chanel?" I asked.

"Daddy, dis DJ."

"What's up, little man?" I asked him. I hadn't been able to spend no time with him at all.

"Daddy, when come see me, 'cause me miss you," DJ asked in his toddler talk.

"I'm going to come and get you tomorrow, and we can go somewhere and go wherever you want to go, okay? Where do you want Daddy to take you?

"Chuck E. Cheese... Can me sisters go, because I want me sisters to go?"

"What do you mean?" I questioned because I knew he couldn't be talking about Alex and Dani.

"Mommy told me, me got sisters."

"What? Let me speak to your mother."

"My mommy not here... me granny here."

"OK, DJ, go give your granny the phone." I could hear DJ running through the house calling for his granny.

"Hey, Damien," Mrs. Charlene said when she got on the phone.

"Hey, Mrs. Charlene. Where's Chanel?" I questioned.

"Damien, that daughter of mine left here this morning, and I haven't heard or seen her since. DJ called her on my cell phone, and that's when we realized she left her cell phone at home." You could hear the aggravation

in Mrs. Charlene's voice because Chanel was a hot ass mess.

"Alright, Mrs. Charlene. I'll take care of you when I see you for keeping DJ all day. When Chanel comes in, tell her to call me, regardless of the time." I wondered what Chanel was up to because her phone was normally glued to her fuckin' ear.

"Fuck!" I heard Bennie yell, and then he threw his phone of the table.

"Nigga, you alright? Do you wanna talk about it?" I asked Bennie. I'd never seen him this upset before.

Bennie leaned back in his chair and looked up at the ceiling like the answers were there. He sat like that for a few minutes before he looked over at me, and by the look in his eye, I could tell he was battling some shit. Hell, I knew the look all too well. I constantly had that mutha-fucka, because I stayed fuckin' up somehow.

"Man... I got so much shit going on right now. I can't even focus fully on what's going on with KDB business because I have so much personal shit hitting me left and right..." Bennie said, and then he ran his hand down his face and let out an exasperated breath.

"Nigga, what got your ass over there looking like me when I found out that Camille knew about me, Chanel, and DJ?" I asked in a jokingly manner. I grabbed my phone and pulled up my text threads and skimmed through a few before I realized Bennie hadn't responded to my joke.

"Man, please don't tell me—Damn, I thought I was the true fuckup out of the group. Nigga, what the fuck did you do, man?" I asked him.

"Well... you know I told you about how I've been

messing around with Diane, but she told me that she's pregnant with my seed today," Bennie said under his breath.

"Ain't no need to get shy now nigga... She's getting an abortion, right?" Bennie gave me a look as if he was disgusted by my comment.

"Man... What the fuck is wrong with you? Why would I want her to kill my fuckin' seed, considering my other two kids died?" He stood up and looked like he was getting ready to beat my ass, but he better rethink that shit because he knows I'm nice as fuck with these hands.

"Hell, I ain't ask you that shit to offend you. I asked you that shit because you're a married fuckin' man, and your side bitch being pregnant gets you a one-way ticket to divorce court or an early grave, my nigga."

"I know. Fuckkk! This shit bad as hell!" he yelled while banging his hand down on the table. A couple of minutes later he calmed that shit down because he knew I was coming from a good place. "She wants to have an abortion, but I'm trying to convince her ass not to. The only way she'll keep it is if we're together raising the baby under one roof. How do I choose between my wife and my seed? After losing multiple kids, my seed has to come before everyone, including myself. This may be my last shot at fatherhood," Ben said, shaking his head. He was in a fucked-up situation, and if I was him, going through all he went through, I didn't know what the fuck I would want her to do either. My situation was different because I already had two living children, so off the top, if it was me, me and my baby mama would have a dinner date at Planned Parenthood!

I heard a knock at the door, and when we looked at

the monitor, we realized it was Mello standing outside the door waiting to be buzzed in. Bennie buzzed him in, and immediately when he walked through the door, he let us know they had chained Chris up in the workroom and that King had just pulled into the parking lot.

I gathered my shit up and headed to my office to change out of the expensive ass, Purple Label outfit and butters I was wearing. Fuckin' with King, you never knew how shit would end up unfolding around you, so it was better to be safe than sorry.

Once I changed my clothes, I headed back downstairs to the workroom. I saw Mello and Wayne standing outside the door chatting it up.

"Why the two of you waiting out here?" I questioned, looking back and forth between the two.

"King asked us to leave, and he said he only wants the heads in there while he takes care of Chris." Wayne informed me.

I didn't respond. I turned toward the door, scanned my thumb on the biometric pad, and punched in my access code. The doors slightly popped open. I headed inside, and Bennie was sitting down at the metal table while King was unchaining Chris's wrist from the thick chain that extended down from the ceiling. I took a seat next to Bennie and watched King get to work.

King didn't say anything. He just walked over to the table we were seated at and took a seat on top of the table, muggin' the hell out of Chris. Chris looked up at King and returned the gesture, like he was hard as hell, but I loved breaking the hard niggas. After a few minutes, Chris burst out laughing. I looked over at this nigga like he was out of his rabbit ass mind.

"What the fuck is so funny!" King yelled. King jumped off the table and two-pieced Chris. Chris ate that shit right up and returned the favor. They were going blow for blow at first because King wasn't putting his all into it, but when Chris hit King in the mouth, King lost his fuckin' mind and was throwing blow after blow after blow until he threw a mean uppercut, which caused Chris to fly up in the air a little and away from King, landing on his back. Bennie and I didn't move a muscle because it was King's show, and if he wanted us to get involved, he would have let us know.

"Nigga, ain't no bitch in my blood!" Chris yelled. He pushed himself off the ground and stood up. After a few seconds, he threw his fists up and got back into a fighting stance. "What? You thought I was going to cry or beg for you to spare my life? Dog, that shit ain't gonna happen either, my nigga." King didn't say anything. He just stared at Chris like he was trying to read his mind or some shit.

"Nigga, I would've never put you on my team if I thought you would fold like that, but answer this question for me, why? Why are you doing all of this?" King questioned while he stared Chris in the eyes giving him a death stare.

"Because you muthafuckas think the world revolves around you, and you can take whatever the fuck you want... and Damien, you're a phony, bitch ass nigga too!" Chris yelled out before he got quiet again, and it was taking everything in me not to get up and stomp a mudhole in his bitch ass.

"Nigga, you ain't put in no work to get to where you are now. All I'm going to say is you killed someone very close to me, and you gotta pay for your sins. Maybe someone will take a gun and place it to Camille's head and pull the trigger, and you'll have to watch her brains being blown out the back of her head and her lifeless body fall to the ground, exactly how I saw it happen to my peoples... I've been watching and waiting for years to get at your ass," Chris said calm as hell like that shit was cool to say.

To stand there and basically threaten my wife's life is a death sentence, but I decided not to let that shit get to me because it wasn't shit. He couldn't do shit to me locked in our workroom, and he wasn't walking out of there alive.

"Are you finished, or are you done?" I arrogantly asked with a chuckle.

"Nah, bitch ass nigga! I ain't done!" Chris started taking steps toward me, so I pushed him back and away from me while still sitting in the chair. This bitch had the nerve pull a glob of spit from his fuckin' lungs and spit it on me, and it landed on my cheek because I was sitting, and he was standing. Now, I don't know how other cities roll, but in Cleveland, spitting on somebody is one of the most disrespectful things you could ever do to somebody. I heard King mumble under his breath, "No, this nigga didn't!"

I saw red and jumped out of my seat and charged at Chris, punching Chris in the face repeatedly until my arm started hurting, and the haymakers I was sending his way were lethal. While punching Chris, I was yelling, "You! Disrespectful! Ass! Bitch!" I said each word in between punches. "You! Disrespectful! Ass! Bitch!" At that point, I blacked out and lost control completely.

"Damien, that's enough," I heard Bennie say after he

lifted me off the ground and walked me away from Chris. I didn't even realized King had come over and started stompin' his ass out too. I knew my nigga felt the disrespect from that shit too, that nasty ass shit. Who the fuck spits on niggas nowadays?

King calmly stopped stompin' Chris and walked away like he ain't probably destroy all that nigga ribs with how he was stomping his ass two seconds ago.

When I looked over at Chris, he was laying on the ground fucked up, but he was still alive. I tried my best to keep my temper at bay because I knew it was very hard to bring me back whenever I went to that dark place, and plus, I had to think like a boss. We needed to get as much information out of Chris as we could, but how bad he looked, I don't think it was much more he was going to say.

"I don't think this nigga gonna say much else, so let's just get this shit over with and blow his muthafuckin' brains out," I said while pulling my gun from behind my back. Both Bennie and King nodded their head in agreement, and as I walking back over toward Chris's body, he was trying to get up off the floor. He was on his hands and knees trying to push his body off the floor but failing miserably.

He was in perfect position once I reached him, and I put my 9mm to his temple, and I was about to pull the trigger, but Chris talking stopped me.

"If you kill me, you'll never find your woman," Chris mumbled out, and I could barely hear him.

"What the fuck did you say?" I questioned.

Chris pushed his body off of the ground and was able to stand, but he was leaning forward some while holding his stomach. He had blood dripping from his mouth, and one of his eyes was already swollen to the point of it being completely shut. We fucked him up badly.

Chris cleared his throat, and then he said, "If you kill me, you'll never find your woman," and that time, I heard him clearly.

He continued, "Y'all bitches was way too busy worrying about the wrong shit, and you left your front doors wide open for me. You didn't find it strange that my intelligent ass was dumb enough to stay here in Cleveland and take shelter in Toy's trifling ass house? Y'all stupid as fuck, and for y'all to be the so-called "real kings of Cleveland" I caught y'all dumb asses slippin'!

"First, the two niggas y'all had watching Sam in the black charger are dead! Second, Sam and Moe are both being held at two undisclosed locations that we both know your team will never find. And my chocolate drop Camille... Camille is at my spot waiting for me naked as the day she was born. Waiting for daddy to come and put this dick in her life," Chris said. I actually threw up in my mouth a little, and he ain't miss a beat. "Damn, Dame you good? Your hotheaded ass shouldn't look so upset."

King ran over to Chris and grabbed him around his neck and asked, "Are you fuckin' serious right now?" We all were looking like pit bulls ready to destroy some shit.

"I take it y'all bitches mad, *mad*, huh?" Chris burst out in a loud cynical laugh, and it was pissing me off because he thought shit was a game, but the situation was further from that. Chris abruptly stopped laughing as King placed the gun to his right temple, and he didn't show an ounce of fear. "Now, the decisions all of you make from this point on will determine how and in what condition the women y'all love will return to you in.

"Y'all probably should answer that," Chris's arrogant as announced as his face held a dumb ass smirk, and it was taking everything in me not to wipe that shit off his face. The crazy part was our phones hadn't even rang yet. That's when it clicked, and our dumb asses played right into his fuckin' hand. He planned this shit out to a tee, and everything played out exactly how Chris planned that shit to, and I already knew he wasn't lying about Sam, Camille, and Moe.

"Fuckkk!" King yelled out.

Ring! Ring! Ring!

All three of us looked at each other, and we knew we had fucked up, and as I looked down at the screen on my phone, I felt weak in the knees when I say Camille's name on the caller ID. The three of us looked at each other, and I already knew what it was. One by one, we all revealed what our caller IDs said.

Bennie said, "It's Moe!"

King shouted, "It's Sam!"

And I yelled, "Fuckkk! It's Camille!"

...TO BE CONTINUED...